Edward E. Hale

Boys' Heroes

Edward E. Hale

Boys' Heroes

ISBN/EAN: 9783337214005

Printed in Europe, USA, Canada, Australia, Japan

Cover: Foto ©Andreas Hilbeck / pixelio.de

More available books at **www.hansebooks.com**

ROBINSON CRUSOE.

BOYS' HEROES

BY

EDWARD EVERETT HALE

ILLUSTRATIONS

BOSTON
D LOTHROP COMPANY
WASHINGTON STREET OPPOSITE BROMFIELD

CONTENTS.

		PAGE.
I.	HECTOR	7
II.	HORATIUS COCLES	26
III.	ALEXANDER THE GREAT	40
IV.	HANNIBAL	51
V.	KING ARTHUR	69
VI.	RICHARD THE LION HEARTED	82
VII.	BAYARD	95
VIII.	ROBINSON CRUSOE	111
IX.	ISRAEL PUTNAM	127
X.	GENERAL LAFAYETTE	137
XI.	NAPOLEON THE FIRST	150
XII.	RALPH ALLESTREE	164

ILLUSTRATIONS.

PAGE.

Robinson Crusoe . . . Frontispiece

Hector and Andromache.— *From the Bas-*
relief by Thorwaldsen . . . 15

"Where stood the Dauntless Three" . 28

"Alone Stood Brave Horatius" . . 31

Alexander the Great 45

King Arthur's Round Table . . . 70

The Sword Excalibar 76

Bayard's Armor 99

The Young Bayard 103

Bartholdi's Statue of Lafayette . . 141

BOYS' HEROES.

I.

HECTOR.

BOYS are jealously exclusive in the choice of their heroes, and have not many.

I asked some of my younger friends why Hector was a boy's hero, to receive these replies:

"Oh, because Achilles was such a hog." Another boy said,

"Oh, you like the Trojans, you know, and you are sorry the Greeks beat them."

I tried to find out whether Hector's gentlemanly traits, of which he has more than any hero of the Iliad, had anything to do with the preference of Hector to Achilles. Do boys like Hector the more because he was kind to Helen — because he

was fond of his wife and his baby? To these questions I have found no satisfactory answers, and I
throw them out for discussion among my young
friends.

Hector had the advantages and the disadvan-
tages of an oldest son. He was the oldest son of
Priam and Hecuba. All along, apparently, he was
befriended by Apollo. I suppose that is a short
way of saying that he was handsome and graceful,
learned his lessons quickly, sung well and danced
well, and got along with the other boys without
frequent rows. I suppose it also means that he
had good health, which is the best thing a boy can
have — that he liked to live in the open air, and
that is the best taste a boy can have. One account
says squarely that he was Apollo's son. But that
is hardly any affair of ours. For our business in
these little papers is chiefly with history.

According to Homer, Priam had fifty sons, of
whom Hecuba was mother of nineteen. Several
of these sons appear in the story, and Alexander or
Paris played the central part in the beginning of it.
But I remember nothing which is said of their edu-

cation, excepting Hector's own statement that he was

—bred to martial pains.

Achilles was specially put under Chiron's care, as if Chiron were a sort of tutor.

Achilles was also "tutored" by Phœnix, to use a very bad word, which is, however, a convenient one. But of Hector's tutors I remember nothing — and schools, I think, were not then invented. Somebody taught him to tell the truth and to fight the enemies of his country. That is the heart of all education, as you will learn when you come to read Amyas Leigh. I think he knew how to read, but of this I am not certain. I doubt if he could spell. But he could run well — only too well. He could swim, I think. He could harness and drive horses. He could play with a baby. He could be good to his wife. Here are all the essentials gained in a good education. As to the question which some readers will think most important — whether he played ball — there can be no doubt that he did. They all played ball, and played

it very well. You will see that Hector, even in the
royal family, could have selected a good nine from
his own brothers, and another nine to play against,
and an umpire. And still there could have been a
good company of brothers and sisters to look on.

When the Greeks landed, it was known by an
oracle that he who landed first would be killed.
Laodamia wrote to her husband Protesiläus,

> Be thine the thousandth of a thousand ships.

But Protesiläus either did not receive the letter or
disregarded it. He was the first Greek to spring
ashore, and Hector was ready and killed him.
So Hector struck the first blow.

You will find this story in "Lucian's Dialogues
of the Dead," an amusing book, in which are a
good many of the later traditions which had grown
up about the older Greek mythology. It is not in
the Iliad. In the Iliad, Hector appears first where
he reproaches Paris, his brother, for running away
from Meneläus. Remember that it is the wife of
Meneläus whom Paris has stolen; and that thus
the whole war began :

As godlike Hector sees the prince retreat
He thus upbraids him with a generous heat;
"Unhappy Paris! but to women brave!
So fairly form'd, and only to deceive!
Oh, hadst thou died when first thou saw'st the light,
Or died at least before thy nuptial rite!
A better fate than vainly thus to boast,
And fly, the scandal of thy Trojan host.
Gods! how the scornful Greeks exult to see
Their fears of danger undeceived in thee!"

Hector then challenged Meneläus himself. Here is the result:

Stung to the heart the generous Hector hears,
But just reproof with decent silence bears.
From his proud car the prince impetuous springs,
On earth he leaps; his brazen armour rings.
Two shining spears are brandish'd in his hands;
Thus arm'd, he animates his drooping bands,
Revives their ardor, turns their steps from flight
And wakes anew the dying flames of fight.
They turn, they stand; the Greeks their fury dare,
Condense their powers and wait the growing war.
. . . . . .
Where Hector march'd, the god of battles shined.
Now storm'd before him, and now raged behind.
. . . . . .

Amazed no less the great Tydides stands:
He stay'd, and turning thus address'd his bands:
"No wonder, Greeks: that all to Hector yield;
Secure of favouring gods, he takes the field;
His strokes they second, and avert our spears;
Behold where Mars in mortal arms appears!
Retire then, warriors, but sedate and slow;
Retire, but with your faces to the foe.
Trust not too much your unavailing might;
'Tis not with Troy, but with the gods ye fight."

There follows a general battle. Even Ares, the god of war, is wounded, as he fights on the Trojan side. Hector goes back to the city to ask his mother to pray to their fast friend, Athene, for relief. It is then he has the interview with his wife Andromache, when the little boy is afraid of the helmet.

Thus having spoke, th' illustrious son of Troy
Stretched his fond arms to clasp the lovely boy.
The babe clung crying to his nurse's breast,
Scared at the dazzling helm and nodding crest.
With secret pleasure each fond parent smiled
And Hector hastened to relieve his child —
The glittering terrors from his brow unbound,
And placed the beaming helmet on the ground;

Then kissed the child, and, lifting high in air,
Thus to the gods preferred a father's prayer:
"O, Thou! whose glory fills the ethereal throne,
And all ye deathless powers, protect my son.
Grant him like me to purchase just renown,
To guard the Trojans, to defend the crown;
Against his country's foes the war to wage
And rise the Hector of a future age.
So, when triumphant from successful toils,
Of heroes slain he bears the reeking spoils,
Whole hosts may hail him with deserved acclaim
And say, this chief transcends his father's fame
While pleased, amidst the general shouts of Troy,
His mother's conscious heart o'erflows with joy."

In the battle which follows Hector is wounded, but
not so severely wounded but that he soon appears
again and again, and when he appears, the Greeks
are apt to be worsted. Then Teucer attacks him,
after having killed eight Trojans in succession by
successful arrow-shots.

"He spoke, and sent another arrow from the
string, aimed at Hector, whom he hoped to strike.
But it missed him, and struck in the heart Gor-
gythion, a brave son of Priam, whose mother was

Castianira, beautiful as a goddess, who had been brought as a slave from Aesyma. And as a poppy in a garden, heavy with its fruit, and supple with the moisture of spring, bends its head upon one side, so bent his heavy head upon one side. And Teucer sent another arrow from the string, aimed at Hector whom he hoped to strike. But even then it missed him, for Apollo warded it off, and it struck Archeptolemus, the brave charioteer of Hector, as he was rushing into the fight—it struck him in the heart. He fell from the chariot, and his horses sprung backward and all his spirit and his strength were gone. And Hector mourned for his charioteer with bitter grief."

I have translated this, almost literally, in the hope that some boy or girl may send to me a version in poetry, half as good as Mr. Sotheby's or a quarter as good as Mr. Pope's. Perhaps a hundred of my readers will try.

You can see here how Hector " turned the scale when he appeared."

As when two scales are charged with doubtful loads,
From side to side the trembling balance nods

(While some laborious matron, just and poor,
With nice exactness weighs her wooly store),
Till, poised aloft, the resting beam suspends
Each equal weight ; nor this, nor that descends :
So stood the war, till Hector's matchless miight
With fates prevailing, turn'd the scale of fight.
Fierce as a whirlwind up the wall he flies,
And fires his host with loud repeated cries :
Advance, ye Trojans ! lend your valiant hands,
Haste to the fleet, and toss the blazing brands.
They hear, they run ; and, gathering at his call,
Raise scaling engines, and ascend the wall :
Around the works a wood of glittering spears
Shoots up, and all the rising host appears.
A ponderous stone bold Hector heaved to throw,
Pointed above, and rough and gross below :
Not two strong men the enormous weight could raise,
Such men as live in our degenerate days.
Yet this, as easy as a swain would bear
The snowy fleece, he toss'd, and shook in air :
For Jove upheld, and lightened of its load
The unwieldy rock, the labour of a god.
Thus arm'd, before the folded gates he came,
Of massy substance, and stupendous frame ;
With iron bars and brazen hinges strong,
On lofty beams of solid timber hung :

Then, thundering through the planks with forceful sway,
Drives the sharp rock; the solid beams give way,
The folds are shatter'd; from the crackling door
Leap the resounding bars, the flying hinges roar.
Now rushing in, the furious chief appears,
Gloomy as night! and shakes two shining spears:
A dreadful gleam from his bright armour came,
And from his eyeballs flashed a living flame.
He moves a god, resistless in his course,
And seems a match for more than mortal force.
Then pouring after, through the gaping space:
A tide of Trojans flows, and fills the place,
The Greeks behold, they tremble, and they fly;
The shore is heaped with dead and tumult fills the sky.

Hector shows himself a fearless leader, and he has the great gift of encouraging his men. Once and again they drive the Grecians — once even to their ships — and Hector with his torch sets fire to them.

Meanwhile Achilles is sulking in his tents. But he permits Patroclus to go out against the Greeks in his armour. Here and now it must be confessed Hector is afraid, and he runs away. This is what I meant when, in my little joke, I said he learned too well how to run. But Apollo encouraged him, he returned to the fight and killed Patroclus. Thus he became the possessor of Achilles' armor. Achilles asked for the body of Patroclus, and Hector refused to surrender it. Polydamas proposes that he should retire into the city. And, for one, knowing the result, I always wished he had done so, from an eager desire to know how, in that case, the Iliad would have ended. But Hector refused. Apollo bade him decline a contest with Achilles — and when Achilles in his new armor came on the field to avenge Patroclus, Priam and Hecuba both implored their son to avoid him, and to retreat. But Hector would not obey. He awaited the Greek hero.

When, however, he saw him, in the terrors of the Vulcan-made armor, his courage failed him. Then was it that he fled three times round the walls of Troy.

> As Hector sees, unusual terrors rise,
> Struck by some god he fears, recedes, and flies.
> He leaves the gates, he leaves the walls behind;
> Achilles follows like the winged wind,

.   .   .   .   the rapid chase they held
One urged by fury, one by fear impelled,

.   .   .   .   .

Swift was the course ; no vulgar prize they play,
No vulgar victim must reward the day,
(Such as in races crown the speedy strife :)
The prize contended was great Hector's life.

.   .   .   .   .

Thus three times round the Trojan wall they fly.
The gazing gods lean forward from the sky ;
To whom, while eager on the chase they look
The·sire of mortals and immortals spoke.

Every boy is indignant as he reads these stories
that the heroes on each side are so heavily "handi-
capped," that is, that just in the crisis of things one
or two gods or goddesses, no better than men or
women, interfere to upset the result which might
have been.   In this particular issue Zeus and
Athene determine that Hector must fall, and Athene even assumes the form of Deiphobus to urge
him to make a stand, which he does and dies.

" 'Tis so — heaven wills it, and my hour is nigh !
I deem'd Deiphobus had heard my call,
But he secure lies guarded in the wall.

A god deceived me; Pallas, 'twas thy deed,
Death and black fate approach! 'tis I must bleed.
No refuge now, no succour from above,
Great Jove deserts me, and the son of Jove,
Propitious once, and kind! Then welcome fate!
'Tis true I perish, yet I perish great:
Yet in a mighty deed I shall expire,
Let future ages hear it and admire!"
Fierce at his word his weighty sword he drew,
And, all collected, on Achilles flew.

. . . .

When all the starry train emblaze the sphere
So shone the point of great Achilles' spear.
In his right hand he waves the weapon round,
Eyes the whole man, and meditates the wound;
But the rich mail Patroclus lately wore,
Securely cased the warrior's body o'er.
One space at length he spies, to let in fate,
Where 'twixt the neck and throat the jointed plate
Gave entrance: through that penetrable part
Furious he drove the well-directed dart:

. . . .

Prone on the field the bleeding warrior lies,
While thus triumphing stern Achilles cries:
" At last is Hector stretch'd upon the plain,
Who feared no vengeance for Patroclus slain:
Then, prince! you should have fear'd, what now you feel.

Achilles absent, was Achilles still;
Yet a short space the great avenger staid,
Then low in dust thy strength and glory laid.
Peaceful he sleeps, with all our rites adorn'd
Forever honor'd and forever mourn'd!"

I suppose that our sympathy for Hector comes
mostly from our feeling that he is quite over-
weighted.   He is almost the only thorough fighter
on the Trojan side.   The Greeks play out such
pieces as Agamemnon, Diomedes, the two Ajaxes,
Ulysses and Achilles himself, and the poor Trojans can only offer this one Hector with any pre-
tence that he equals them.   Now we always take
the side of a person so over-matched.   Then we
like him because he does think of other things
than blood and carnage.   He can kiss his wife and
play with his baby.   And we like him because
Achilles treated him so badly—or, as my young
friend said, "because Achilles was such a hog!"

High o'er the slain the great Achilles stands,
Begirt with heroes and surrounding bands;
And thus aloud, while all the host attends;
Princes and leaders! countrymen and friends!

Is not Troy fallen already? Haste, ye powers!
See if already their deserted towers
Are left unmanned; or if they yet retain
The souls of heroes, their great Hector slain.
Meanwhile, ye sons of Greece, in triumph bring,
The corpse of Hector, and your pæans sing.
Be this the song, slow-moving toward the shore,
" Hector is dead, and Ilion is no more."
Then his fell soul a thought of vengeance bred
(Unworthy of himself, and of the dead);
The nervous ancles bored, his feet he bound
With thongs inserted through the double wound;
These fix'd up high behind the rolling wain,
His graceful head was trail'd along the plain.
Proud on his car the insulting victor stood,
And bore aloft his arms, distilling blood.
He smites the steeds; the rapid chariot flies;
The sudden clouds of circling dust arise.
Now lost is all that formidable air;
The face divine, and long-descending hair,
Purple the ground, and streak the sable sand;
Deform'd, dishonor'd, in his native land,
Given to the rage of an insulting throng,
And, in his parent's sight, now dragg'd along!

Here is Priam's prayer as he begged Achilles to
surrender the body.

Think, O Achilles, semblance of the gods,
On thine own father, full of days like me,
And trembling on the gloomy verge of life.
Some neighbour chief, it may be, even now
Oppresses him, and there is none at hand,
No friend to succor him in his distress.
Yet, doubtless, hearing that Achilles lives
He still rejoices, hoping day by day,
That one day he shall see the face again
Of his own son, from distant Troy returned.
But me no comfort cheers, whose bravest sons,
So late the flower of Ilium, are all slain.
When Greece came hither, I had fifty sons;
But fiery Mars hath thinned them.—One I had,
One, more than all my sons, the strength of Troy,
Whom standing for his country, thou hast slain—
Hector.   His body to redeem I come
Into Achaia's fleet, bringing myself,
Ransom inestimable to thy tent.
Rev'rence the gods, Achilles! recollect
Thy father; for his sake compassion show
To me more pitiable still, who draw
Home to my lips (humiliation yet
Unseen on earth,) his hand who slew my son!

How sweetly Helen mourned him. Of all the
heroes he was the one who had been good to her.

Oh Hector! thou wert rooted in my heart;

No brother there had half so large a part.

Not less than twenty years are now passed o'er,

Since first I landed on the Trojan shore,

Since Paris lured me from my home away.

(Would I had died before that fatal day!)

Yet it was ne'er my fate from thee to find

A deed ungentle, or a word unkind.

When others cursed the authoress of their woe,

Thy pity checked my sorrows in their flow:

If by my sisters or the queen reviled,

(For the good king, like thee, was ever mild)

Thy kindness still has all my grief beguil'd.

For thee I mourn, and mourn myself in thee,

Nor hope, nor solace now remains to me;

Sad Helen has no friend, now thou art gone.

II.

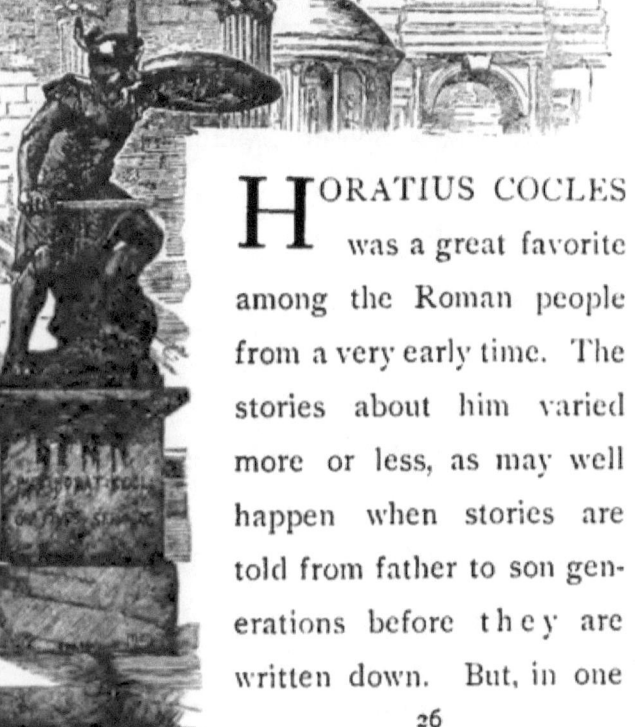

HORATIUS COCLES was a great favorite among the Roman people from a very early time. The stories about him varied more or less, as may well happen when stories are told from father to son generations before t h e y are written down. But, in one

26

form or another, every historian of early Rome tells the tale.

The historian Niebuhr suggested that the stories we have of early Roman history must have been, at one time or another, transmitted in the form of ballads. And, with a great deal of ingenuity, and a great deal of spirit, Mr. Macaulay reproduced some of these supposed ballads from the history. These he called *Lays of Ancient Rome,* and they have awakened, for this generation, an interest wholly new in the stories. Mr. Macaulay himself, indeed, is more likely to be remembered, two hundred years hence, on their account, than for anything else which he has written.

So is it that almost every schoolboy who will read this article, has read, and perhaps has told from the platform on "Declamation Day," that

> Then out spake brave Horatius
> The Captain of the Gate,
> "To every man upon this earth
> Death cometh, soon or late.
> And how can man die better
> Than facing dreadful odds

For the ashes of his fathers,
And the temples of his Gods!"

It would be rather an interesting thing to compare the different stories about the three who held

"WHERE STOOD THE DAUNTLESS THREE."

the bridge, as they were told by the different historians of repute.   Any boy or girl who lives where
there is a good public library can do this, easily
enough, by looking out the article "Horatius
Cocles" in Smith's larger *Dictionary of Biography*,
and then finding the authorities cited there.   Some
of them have been translated into English, and for

the rest, the boys who are studying Latin could hammer out the meaning without much difficulty. Indeed, that would not be a bad subject to give to a bright class at school for a "composition" to show the difference between the various narratives of "The Battle at the Bridge."

Here is the story as Plutarch tells it :

Porsenna, making a sharp assault, obliged the defenders to retire to Rome. In their entrance they had almost admitted their enemy into the city with them. But Publicola, by sallying out at the gate, prevented them. He joined battle by the side of Tiber — and opposed the enemy as they pressed on with great multitudes — but at last he sank under desperate wounds and was carried out of the fight. The same fortune befell Lucretius, so that the Romans in dismay retreated into the city for safety, and Rome was in great hazard of being taken, for the enemy forced their way upon the wooden bridge over Tiber. But Horatius Cocles, seconded by Herminius and Lartius, who were two of the first men of Rome, made head against them. Horatius had the name of Cocles, from the loss of one of his eyes in the wars — or, as others write, from the depression in his nose — which left nothing in the middle to separate the two eyes — and thus made both his eyes to appear as one : — hence, meaning to say Cyclops, by a mispronunciation they called him Cocles.

This Cocles kept the bridge, and held back the enemy till his own party broke it down behind, and then with his armour dropped into the river, and swam to the hither side, with a wound in his hip from a Tuscan spear.*

Publicola, admiring his courage, proposed at once that the Romans should every one make him a present of a day's provisions, and afterwards give him as much land as he could plough around in one day, and besides, erected a brazen statue to his honor in the temple of Vulcan, as a requittal for the lameness caused by his wound.

This statue, it would appear, remained visible to a late period in Roman history.

All this happened when the republic was newly formed, Publicola being, indeed, one of the first two consuls. The name of Horatius is enough to show that Cocles was one of the great Horatian family. which appears very early in history and lasted till after the Empire began. The poet Horace was connected with it in some way; and every boy named "Horace" may look to it as having given him his name. So we know that Horatius Cocles was, in a fashion, a relation of the three Horatii.

* This is one of Plutarch's frequent absurdities. Cyclops is a Greek word, and there was no reason why the Romans should speak Greek.

"ALONE STOOD BRAVE HORATIUS."

Now it may have been that the Horatian family, or *gens*, as it is the rather affected fashion to call it now, was specially prolific of brave men, ready to die for their country. Or it may be, that, some fifty or a hundred years after, there was some bard among the retainers of the family or in the family itself, who was specially good in composing and singing the lays of old times. In that case there would be more Lays of the Horatian family than of any other, and their lays would have lasted longer.

Mr. Macaulay, in his ballad, clings very closely to this story. He gives to it the confirmation of the statue.

And, in all such things, a visible statue is a great help to the man who sings the song.

> And they made a molten image
> And set it up on high,
> And there it stands until this day
> To witness if I lie.
> It stands in the Comitium,
> Plain for all folk to see,
> Horatius in his harness
> Halting upon one knee.

> And underneath is written
> In letters all of gold,
> How valiantly he kept the bridge
> In the brave days of old.

The poet Horace himself says that "brave men lived before Agamemnon;" and he says that the reason why no one remembered them was that they had no Homer to write about them.

> Swords flashed and lances flew, armor rung
> Before Atrides fought or Homer sung.

This is a hint to people who would build up the reputation of their families, that they will do well not to spend so much money on perishable marble, and to do more to encourage the young poets of the household.

Horatius Cocles is the hero who represents men who have had to stand alone for their country. And he is not simply a selected champion for his country, as David is when he kills Goliath, or as Hector is when he fights Achilles before the walls of Troy. As the story is told, the whole fate of his country "pivots" upon him. Now this is often the case when people do not know that it is so. The wise man saves the city, and no one thanks him for saving it. But the instances are few in history where in a picturesque and distinct way one man so stands out that you see that his success is the success of his country and that his fall is his country's fall.

We remember Arnold von Winkelried as such a man, but the crisis is less than in Horatius' success. Jane Darc, the Maid of Orleans, may be spoken of in that way. While she succeeded, France succeeded. When she failed, France failed. But here is rather an instance where the country needed a leader and found one. In the case of Horatius it is not a leader who was needed; Publicola was a sufficient leader. Horatius had a great opportunity and he was suffcient for it. When John Hampden took the whole shock of the anger and harm of the king, he was such a man. But Hampden was only one of many who in turn would have taken the same stand. Hampden's case was the first one on trial, and with the sturdy pluck which distinguishes Englishmen, he stood the assault, although it were led by his king. In American history Mr. Joshua

Giddings is somewhat such a man. He represented the People at a time when the lower House of Congress did not want to hear the People. Then the House would turn him out. The People would elect him again. The House would turn him out again. The time came when the People again controlled the House, and to that time I suppose he had looked forward.

But as I said before, it is only because we do not see very deeply into the causes of things that we see but few such picturesque instances and preserve the names of but few of such heroes. The proverb says that "for want of a nail the shoe was lost, and for want of a shoe the horse was lost, and for want of a horse the rider was lost, and for want of a rider the army was lost, and for want of an army the crown was lost, and all for the want of a two-penny nail." But that seems to me but a bleak way of telling history.

I like to begin at the other end, and to work forward and upward. I would tell the story thus:

There was a boy whom we will name Luke Varnum. He was fifteen years old, and he was lame of

his left foot. So when every other boy in Number
Five, and every man, old and young, shouldered
his firelock and marched off to join General Stark,
and go and fight the Hessians at Bennington, Luke
was left at home. He limped out and held the
stirrup for Lieutenant Chittinden to mount, and
then he had to stay at home with the babies and
the women.

The men had been gone an hour and a half when
three men galloped up on horseback. And Luke
went down to the rails to see who they were. " Is
there nobody here ? " said one of them.

" Yes," said Luke, " I am here."

" I see that," said the first man, laughing. " What
I mean is, is there nobody here can set a shoe ? "

" I think I can," said Luke. " I often tend fire
for Jonas. I can blow the bellows, and I can hold
the horse's foot. Anyway, I will start up the
fire."

So Luke went into the forge and took down the
tinder-box and struck a light. He built the fire,
and hunted up half a dozen nails which Jonas had
left unintentionally, and he had even made two

more when a fourth horseman came slowly down
on a walk.

"What luck," said he, "to find a forge with the
fire lighted!"

"We found one," said Marvin, "with a boy who
knew how to light it." And the other speaker flung
himself off the horse meanwhile.

And Luke pared the hoof of the dainty creature,
and measured the shoe, which was too big for her.
He heated it white, and bent it closer, to the proper
size. "It is a poor fit," he said, "but it will do."

"It will do very well," said her rider. "But she
is very tender-footed, and I do not dare trust her
five miles unshod."

And for pride's sake, the two first nails Luke
drove were those he had made himself. And when
the shoe was fast, he said: "Tell Jonas that I het
up the forge — and put on the shoe."

"We will tell him," said the Colonel, laughing,
and he rode on. But one of the other horsemen
tarried a minute, and said, "Boy, no ten men who
left you to-day have served your country as you
have. It is Colonel Warner."

When I read in the big books of history how
Colonel Warner led up his regiment just in time to
save the day at Bennington, I am apt to think of
Luke Varnum.

When I read that that day decided the battle of
Saratoga, and that Saratoga determined that America should be independent, I think of Luke Varnum.

When I go to see monuments erected in memory of Colonel Warner, and General Stark, and
even poor old Burgoyne, I think of Luke Varnum
and others like him.

And then sometimes I wonder whether every
man and boy of us who bravely and truly does the
very best thing he knows how to do, does not have
the future of the world resting on him.   If it be so
there are, all unknown in the world, a good many
persons like Horatius Cocles.

III.

ALEXANDER THE GREAT.

BOYS and girls are glad to see young people come forward well, when they read history. There are four or five people in the history of the world, who have set it forward in young life, and have shown that much may be entrusted to young life which is generally left to persons far advanced. Alexander the Great died when he was thirty-two; but he had wholly changed the history of the world before he died. Raphael died when he was thirty-six; Lord Byron died when he was thirty-six.

When I was a boy, every boy in college knew that William Pitt was in Parliament when he was twenty-one, was Chancellor of the Exchequer when twenty-two, and that he was Prime Minister of England before he was twenty-four years old. I remember a college poem of mine, written when I

was only seventeen, in which were the following
lines :

> Will youthful ardor youth's success permit?
> Search through all history, find **one** only Pitt.

The lines were certainly unfortunate. For the
most interesting thing about this William Pitt is
that he was son of the other William Pitt —
that both father and son were prime ministers —
the elder being the greatest minister England ever
had. But what I meant, in the couplet, was that
the younger was the only prime minister England had had so young. And this was true.
There have been plenty of "royal favorites" as
young, but they were not, strictly, ministers. I
have lived long enough also, to know that it is a
great pity for the world that there was more than
one Pitt, and that this particular Pitt ever was
prime minister. The world would be much better
off to-day, I think, had he spent his life in making
heads to pins, or in spinning cotton, as I believe
he should have done on the crack theory of Political Economy.

To go back to Alexander, he and Raphael and

Byron will always be favorites among young people.
Young people feel that it would be a nice thing if
the world were entrusted more to them. I remember that, a few years ago, some spirited boys engaged Faneuil Hall, in Boston, for a meeting to
make a protest against the statute which prohibits
them from voting in Massachusetts — where they
are permitted to hurrah and carry torches.

When Alexander came to the front, this fascina-
ting theory of youth was put to a critical test —
and it succeeded wonderfully well. For so long as
Alexander was very young, he succeeded. And
he had passed thirty, that is, he had entered on
what young people call middle life, before his
great failure.

Alexander's life illustrates another thing — the
good of having a first-rate father and mother, and
the good of first-rate education. "He inherited
from Philip," says Dr. Smith, "his cool foresight
and practical wisdom, and from Olympias his
mother, her ardent enthusiasm." These are excellent things to inherit. Ardent enthusiasm and
cool foresight are a combination as good as one

could ask, for a start on successful life. Dr. Smith adds, alas, that he inherited "ungovernable passions from Olympias, also." Some of us think that no passions are ungovernable. But it was the misfortune of poor Alexander that he did not know that Spirit, by whose alliance only, such passions are to be governed.

His mother was of the royal family of Epirus, in the northern part of what is now the little modern kingdom of Greece. Alexander was fond of claiming descent, through her, from Achilles. I do not see any reason for supposing that he was not right in this claim. What is certain is that her great-grandfather was King of Epirus; and the traditions of Achilles say that his son Pyrrhus, or Neoptolemus, was King of Epirus. Between Pyrrhus and Olympias would come six or seven hundred years — perhaps twenty generations. But there is no reason why the genealogy of the kings of that country should not be kept as well for those generations as the genealogies were kept for the twenty generations between Egbert King of England and the Wars of the Roses. Alexander cer-

tainly had a better chance to know than you and
I have. And I offer this as a good rule in forming an opinion on any point of history — that sensible men, at or near the time of action, had many
opportunities for knowing the truth which people
cannot have one thousand years, or two thousand
or more years away. This rule will seem common-
place, but it is, in truth, very generally scorned.

If I had to write the life of Alexander, in one
hundred words, I should say that he had a good
education, and profited by it. When he was only
sixteen, Philip, his father, left him in charge of
Macedonia while he was at war. Four years after,
Philip died, leaving Alexander king. He was surrounded by enemies. But he marched North, and
conquered the barbarians, South, and conquered
the Greeks and then, with the aid of all of them
but the Lacedæmonians, he overran Asia Minor,
Syria and Egypt and conquered Persia. He afterwards marched into India, but did not remain there.
He made Babylon his capital and died there at
the age of thirty-two.

But when I asked my young friend, Tom Haliday, to write a life of Alexander, after he had been reading Plutarch for an hour, Tom produced this memoir, and I found he had used up his hundred

ALEXANDER THE GREAT.

words long before the young man came to his throne.

"There came a man called Philanicus who had a beautiful white horse, which he offered for thirteen talents. But when they tried him, he proved to be so vicious that no one dared to ride him.

Then Alexander spoke up, and said that it was a
great shame that they should lose such a beautiful
horse for want of a man to ride him. The people
all laughed at him, when he said that he could
manage him better than any of them, and they told
him he could try.

"Alexander walked up to him, and turned his
head towards the sun, for he had observed that it
was his own shadow that he was afraid of. He
then threw off his upper garments and gave a
spring into the saddle and started him at full
speed."

To tell you the truth, I think Tom's method of
writing history more entertaining than mine. And
the reason why Plutarch's *Lives* have been read by
almost all people who could read, now for fifteen
hundred and more years since they were written, is
that they are all crowded full of just such stories
of separate incidents, well wrought out in detail.
They do not undertake to give a philosophical
view of the man's life, so much as to give some
very vivid pictures of separate incidents in it. One
of Plutarch's *Lives* is thus a sort of picture gallery.

with several pictures of curious or important events. But a regularly-built biography of the modern fashion is more like a map, on which the various things are put down in proper relation to each other. It is however, all the same, by no means so attractive at the first sight, and there is a certain reality given a picture to which no map can pretend.

Philip, the father of Alexander, had made such preparation as he could for the invasion of Asia. The Greeks had never forgotten the invasions by Darius and Xerxes. There was a permanent quarrel, indeed, between Greece and Persia. And you must remember that Persia held Asia Minor, and drew tribute even from the Greek cities on its Western coast. So that when Alexander crossed the Bosphorus to the field of Troy, he was in the same old contest with which in the *Iliad*, Greek history and poetry began — the history in which our friend Hector played his part so well. First, Paris crosses to Greece, and steals Helen. Then Greece confederates against Troy, crosses to Asia and destroys Troy. Then, after five or six centuries, in which there have been many raids, backwards and forwards, Darius makes the greatest raid of all, comes down upon the Greeks, and is defeated at Marathon. Ten years after, Xerxes tries again and is defeated at Salamis. The next year, the great Persian fleet is destroyed at Mycale. The march of the ten thousand, when the younger Cyrus attempts to take possession of the Persian throne, is a Greek effort to retaliate — so far as the ten thousand are concerned. This was seventy-nine years after Salamis; and sixty-seven years after this, Alexander pays off the Greek debt entirely, or begins to. He crosses into Asia in the year 334 before Christ, and thirteen years after, at the battle of Arbela, takes possession of the Persian Empire. These thirteen years distinctly changed the history of the world.

I remember that I used to wonder why when he had well-conquered Babylon, he never went home to Macedonia. The answer is, that he and his men were too much fascinated by Eastern luxury. The tide of Empire may take its way Westward, but the longings for luxury always turn Eastward. You have heard Mr. Appleton's joke, that good Americans go to Paris when they die. You have noticed perhaps, that rich Californians go to New York and Paris and Rome to spend their money. So when Mark Antony took possession of Alexandria, Alexandria took possession of him. And, in just this way, when Alexander and his rough Greeks found themselves in the luxuries of Babylon, they were just like these unfortunate Americans, who will read these lines in the comforts and luxuries of Italy or Germany or France, and shudder when they find that I or any other cynic think they would be much better off at home.

When I was a schoolboy, there was a dialogue in the schoolbooks, in which Alexander was represented as a "Thracian robber." The boys stood in attitudes represented in a picture, and the dialogue ended by Alexander's saying penitently, "Alexander a robber? let me reflect." The piece was the outgrowth of a sort of sentimental philosophy which was in vogue a hundred years ago, and it will certainly not stand any fair criticism. Wherever Alexander went, he left something better than he found. He admitted Egypt into the circulation of

the Mediterranean System by building Alexandria.
He introduced India to the knowledge of the Western World. He made easy and systematic the com-
munications between Europe and Asia. Thought-
ful persons are used to say that in the time of our
Saviour, Palestine was the very centre of the Old
World. It was so. It was the place from which the
Infinite Revelation of Absolute Religion could most
easily go out to the world. It was so, because
Alexander had established his empire. If it were
only that he made the Greek language the language
of the civilization of those centuries — in that single
change Alexander would have changed history.

"The conquests of Alexander," says Mr. Samuel
Eliot, "smoothed the way for the chariot wheels of
the Gospel."

IV.

HANNIBAL.

WHEN making a list of the heroes who interest intelligent boys, I consulted many
friends, but we did not always agree. But I think
they all said that Hannibal should be on the list,
yet I think none of them said why. I believe he
stands out in the memory of boys who have read
more or less of Roman history, as none of the men
do who were opposed to him; though many of these
were certainly great men, and though we know
much more of them than we know of him. Fabius,
Marcellus, Cornelius Scipio, for instance, are all of
them men remarkable for what they were and what
they did; they fill important places in Roman history; their lives are fully and well written. But I
do not think any one would name them on a list of
boys' heroès.

I should account for this fondness for Hannibal, wherever it exists, chiefly by the fact that he beat the Romans so often, and kept them under so long. It is just as one likes Hector, because being on the weaker side he held his own so well against the Greeks who in the end were to crush him and his. Doctor Johnson says you cannot see two dogs fighting without sympathizing with one dog or the other. If this is true, I think right-minded people would generally sympathize with the weaker dog, supposing that neither dog had forfeited sympathy. This is certain, that as schoolboys wade along through the rather dull history of the Roman republic, which, as taught them, is only a chronicle of five centuries of war, they tire of the steady story of brute success. It is like watching a pile-driver all day long, as it knocks the piles down into the mud. You would be glad to have one pile rebel and refuse to go down. So, when Brennus at the head of his Gauls, or Hannibal at the head of his Carthaginians, turns the tide of luck for a few years, you are much obliged to them if it were only that they bring some variety into a tedious story.

Then there is the pretty incident, where his father takes him as a little boy to the altar of his country, and makes him swear hostility to Rome. You and I, who are still boys, like to think that a boy can make up his mind, early in life, what he will do, and what he will be, that he can keep on the lines he proposed then, and come out triumphantly, as for nearly thirty years at least after his vow Hannibal did.

The little story is certainly true. And I suppose there were plenty of people in Carthage who held to a peace policy. I suppose they said that this hatred of the Romans was a very old-fashioned prejudice. I suppose they said that a new generation of Romans had grown up, that they were amiable Romans and good Romans, and that they spoke the Carthaginian language quite well, and that they liked to buy the Carthaginian figs and that, in short, they were very different Romans from the Romans whom Hannibal's father hated, and whom the little boy had sworn to overthrow. But Hannibal did not believe such people when he came to be a man. He had found out, somehow or other, what is the only secret of success, namely, that only he who endures to the end shall be saved.

He did not mean to have his nation put up with little aggressions or great aggressions. He did not mean to have Rome cut in on her colonies or interfere with her citizens in their trade. Up and down the Mediterranean he meant that the prestige of a Carthaginian citizen should be as good as that of a Roman citizen. And he would have gained this, if his people had stood by him.

Some people will tell you that they failed because theirs was a mercantile state, and their government the government of merchants. It has been quite the fashion in England, for the last thirty years, for grumblers to say this, and to warn England that if her government is carried on in the interests of merchants, she will go to destruction as Carthage did. You will find England called the "modern Carthage" in satires and philippics. But I do not believe it can be proved that Carthage failed because she was governed by merchants. On the other hand I think that the resources which Carthage had gained from mercantile adventure,

such as the gold and silver and tin and copper and
iron which her seamen brought her from distant
mines, with the skill of those seamen, and the vigor
of her adventurers — I think that these gave her the
means to carry on the struggle with Rome. Rome
was not what we should call a mercantile power
but a military power. That is, the first thought of
each citizen was not trade but art.

I have said the Carthaginians failed because they
could not hold on. Their policy was vacillating.
They deserted Hannibal who never deserted them.
They could not endure to the end. If anybody
wants to know why they finally went to pieces and
disappeared in the long struggle with Rome, he
must find out why they could not hold on.

Well, the answer to that question is the same
which you have when you ask the same question
about the people of Jericho and Ai and all the
Canaanites whom Joshua and his army found in
Palestine, a thousand years before the time of Hannibal. Those people were of the same race as the
Carthaginians, who in fact emigrated from Tyre —
some people think because the Israelites pressed

them in Southern Syria — and they sought new homes when they were crowded out. When Virgil calls Dido " Elissa," we ought to remember it was the same name as " Jezebel " who was Dido's relative, and could have understood her if they could have met. Now the Canaanites could not hold on. They could not stand against the persistent pressure of the Israelites though their armor were as good, their tactics as good and though they fought for their homes.

The weakness of Carthaginians and Canaanites is here. Such worship as they had — it would be a shame to call it religion — is a worship of things that they see. Instead of what we call morals, instead of right and wrong, their rulers, teachers, priests are seeking personal physical enjoyment. Nobody cares for the word "OUGHT" or for the reality it expresses. Each man cares for what pleases his taste, his eye, his ear, or some of his senses. This is what is meant when it is said they worship Belial, and Moloch and Thammuz, while it is said that the conquering Hebrews worship an unknown God who has no name but " I AM."

Now the Romans were not people who made a great deal of the external observances of worship, though they did not neglect them. But they did make a great deal of the word " Right," and of the idea in the word "Ought." When Regulus went back to Carthage to die, because he had said he would, he showed the Carthaginians something which they did not understand or comprehend. A Carthaginian would have lied under these circumstances. The Carthaginian would have elected present comfort. The Roman had an idea of eternal truth. The Roman therefore in the days of the Republic could endure to the end.

Hannibal was the son of Hamilcar Barca, a Carthaginian chief who hated the Romans, and led the Carthaginian party which insisted on war with them. Hannibal was born in the very year when his father was appointed to the Carthaginian forces in Sicily. He did not succeed there, and the Carthaginians lost Sicily. Hamilcar went to Spain afterwards as the Carthaginian commander there. He took the boy Hannibal with him, though he was but nine years old. And it was then that he made him

swear eternal hatred to the Romans at the altar in
Carthage.   Hannibal never forgot this.   He told
the story of it to Antiochus, not long before his own
death.   Here is his own account of it:

When I was a little boy not more than nine years old, my
father offered sacrifices to Jupiter the Best and Greatest, on
his departure from Carthage as general in Spain.   While he
was conducting the sacrifice, he asked me if I would like to
go to the camp with him.   I said I would gladly, and began
to beg him not to hesitate to take me.   He replied, " I will
do it if you will make the promise I demand."   He took me
at once to the altar, at which he had offered his sacrifice, he
bade me take hold of it, having sent the others away, and
bade me swear that I would never be in friendship with the
Romans.

To this boy's vow he was always true.   He could
not have had a better school for war than was
Spain, nor a better teacher than his father.   The
Carthaginians were establishing their colonies in
the southern part of Spain, the Romans were
strengthening their allies in the northern part.   The
river Ebro, which they called Iberus, had been
agreed upon as a dividing line between the two em-

pires. The Spanish tribes were by no means easy
under their foreign rulers, and were constantly re-
belling. Hannibal loved the open air, and he loved
war. He was indifferent to personal luxury. He
did not sleep because it was night, but because his
work was done. He did not rise from bed because
it was morning, but because he had something to
do. So they say he was indifferent to day or night.
His dress was always simple, but his arms and his
horses were always of the best. When he was so
young as to be under command, he was always a
favorite with his superiors, and then and afterwards
he was always a favorite with his army. It seems
to have been taken for granted from the beginning
that he was to be a great commander. He commanded the Carthaginian cavalry when he was
eighteen years old, and took command of the whole
army on his father's death, when he was hardly
twenty-five or twenty-six. When he took his army
across the Alps, he was hardly older than Napoleon
was when he did the same thing twenty centuries
after.

So soon as he had an army at his command he

pounced on Saguntum, a city in alliance with the
Romans. Saguntum had been founded by Greek
colonists who came from Zacynthus, from which it
derives its name. There is a Spanish village at the
place now called Murviedro, which word is the re-
mainder of the Latin words *Muri veteres*, " the old
walls." After a most obstinate defence, Saguntum
was totally destroyed and Hannibal immediately
proceeded to march against Rome.

He propitiated the tribes in Gaul who did not
like the Romans any too well. He crossed the
Rhone with his army in face of the advance guard
of the Romans. It is a great military problem how
to cross a great river in face of an enemy, and any
boy will be interested in seeing how Hannibal
brought his large army forward, especially his forty
elephants. Keeping well inland so as to avoid the
Roman army near the coast, he approached the
Alps which he was determined to cross before winter. His success in bringing his army over, though
with loss, is regarded as one of the great achieve-
ments in war.

Livy's account of it is picturesque. But I — who

sometimes believe that I have been over the same
pass, at the same season of the year, namely October — think Livy made his account rather from
some hard experiences of his own in the mountains,
than from any chronicles which had lasted two
hundred and fifty years.   It is in this story that the
famous account comes in of their cutting through
the rocks by heating them and pouring on vinegar.

The soldiers being then set to make a way down the cliff,
by which alone a passage could be effected, and it being necessary that they should cut through the rocks, having felled,
and lopped, a great number of large trees which grew around,
they made a huge pile of timber ; and as soon as a strong
wind fit for exciting the flames arose, they set fire to it, and,
pouring vinegar on the heated stones, they render them soft
and crumbling. They then open a way with iron instruments
through the rock thus heated by the fire, and soften its de-
clivities by gentle windings, so that not only the beasts of
burden, but also the elephants, could be led down it.

Now if you ask me what I think about this, I
should say that Hannibal was a much better engineer than Livy.   He undoubtedly had with his
army the best engineers of the time who knew the

best processes of the time for quarrying and re-
ducing rock.   Given the problem which was to improve the mountain trail, so that an army of seventy
thousand men might descend from the summit in
four days, they undoubtedly did things that very
much surprised the natives.   Among those things
such enterprises as this of heating and cracking
rock would have been most likely to be remembered by tradition.   And, if the use of vinegar or
any other acids came into the quarrying of that
time, the mountaineers would very naturally have
remembered it.

But I should not advise any member of the Ap-
palachian Club who wanted to improve the pass
through Carter's Notch, which in my judgment
needs improvement, to rely on a bottle of vinegar.

By the time the army was in the plains of Lombardy, it was much reduced.   Hannibal had started
from Saguntum with a good force, but he had sent
back many, some I suppose had deserted in Gaul,
and in the passes of the Alps he had lost great
numbers. What he had, however, were picked men,
and in the spring, refreshed by their winter in the

country, they met Flaminius with his army of Romans. The Carthaginians were hardened and trained by their winter's experience. The Romans, though they had been worsted at Trebia and the Po, were confident with true Roman conceit. But they had been recruited at a time, when, according to Livy, the Romans were more sunk in sloth and unfit for war than ever. Flaminius himself was headstrong and rash, and Hannibal fooled him to his ruin. When you go to Italy, you will not find it hard to see the " reedy lake of Thrasymene " where the Roman army was ruined and Flaminius killed. You can see it from the railway as you ride from Florence to Rome. Here is Lord Byron's description :

I roam
By Thrasimene's lake, in the defiles
Fatal to Roman rashness, more at home ;
For there the Carthaginian's warlike wiles
Come back before me, as his skill beguiles
The host between the mountains and the shore,
Where Courage falls in her despairing files,
And torrents, swollen to rivers with their gore,
Reek through the sultry plain, with legions scattered o'er.

.   .   .   .

Far other scene is Thrasimene now;
Her lake a sheet of silver, and her plain
Rent by no ravage save the gentle plough;
Her aged trees rise thick as once the slain
Lay where their roots are; but a brook hath ta'en —
A little rill of scanty stream and bed —
A name of blood from that day's sanguine rain;
And Sanguinetto tells you where the dead
Made the earth wet, and turn'd the unwilling waters red.

The Roman people were like all nations who have not had recent experience of war at home, and when they saw their legions march out well-appointed, they had been quite sure of victory. Of a sudden one straggler returning, announced what they could not bear to believe, that their consul was dead and their army routed. It was then and thus that this city of Rome began to feel the pressure of that long war which lasted sixteen years, while Hannibal ravaged one part of Italy and another. It was the beginning of the training which was to cure Rome, for the moment, of her luxury and to lift her, for the time, from her degeneracy.

You have heard it said that the luxuries of

Capua, the chief city of Campania, were really what defeated Hannibal. It has become a proverbial expression to say of any luxury which destroys a successful man, that it is his "Capua." But I think the best opinion of the best military men relieves Hannibal from the charge implied in this sneer. It is very easy for you and me, sitting at our ease here two thousand and one hundred years after all this happened, to say that, after routing the Roman army at Thrasymene, he should have marched directly on Rome and destroyed it. But he certainly knew his business better than we do. He passed by Rome into Campania, and made his headquarters for a time at Capua. For the next fifteen years and more he did very much what he chose in Italy, often advancing to the very walls of Rome, but never strong enough to storm a city where by this time every man was a soldier, nor to blockade it so as to starve it into submission. In this time he partially regained the command of Sicily, which the Carthaginians had lost after the first Punic War. He was cruelly disappointed and the fate of the world was changed when Claudius Nero, the Roman commander in the north of Italy, defeated Hasdrubal, Hannibal's brother, who was bringing him reinforcements. Nero sent Hasdrubal's head into Hannibal's camp, and when he saw it, he sighed and said, " I see the fate of Carthage."

The end came when Cornelius Scipio built a Roman fleet, carried an army across to Africa and threatened Carthage itself. It is from this bold enterprise that we take our proverb, " He carried the war into Africa." The Carthaginian senate could not endure to the end. They began sending for Hannibal, who at first would not come. At last he came and the great battle of Zama followed, one of the critical battles of the history of the world. Whatever advantage the Carthaginians had was in their cavalry. Their force of infantry was inferior to that of the Romans. But the Romans had for allies the Numidians, people who lived in the country which we now call Morocco. It is one of the most productive countries in the world. If it had a decent government, it would be the granary of Europe to-day. Now the Numidian horse and their force of elephants were more than a match for those of the Carthaginians. The battle began by a conflict in which the Numidians swept the Carthaginian cavalry out of the field. The Roman infantry then pressed on the Carthaginian infantry. They stood the attack at first, but when the Numidian cavalry returned and joined in the attack, the Carthaginian army gave way — and Hannibal's career of victory was ended.

He told the Carthaginian senate that all was lost, and they made such terms as Romans would grant to the conquered. Poor Hannibal could not long remain in Carthage. He was one of the chief magistrates there for a year or two. But one party there hated him worse than the Romans hated him. He, however, addressed the people of Carthage and taught them that it was necessary. He said in his first address to them, " having left you when nine years old I have returned after an absence of thirty-six years." He had never been in his own country since he was a child.

He knew that the Romans would wish to make him a prisoner. He sailed at once to Syria, where he entrusted himself to Antiochus the Third, one of

the successors, after nearly a century, of Alexander
the Great. He served Antiochus faithfully till the
Romans so pressed him that he was forced to give
up his guest and Hannibal retired to Bithynia.
Here again the Romans followed him up. They
could not be at ease while he lived, and Flaminius
was sent to Prusias, King of Bithynia, to demand
his surrender. Prusias was mean enough to send
troops for his arrest. When Hannibal found his
escape was cut off, he took poison and died.

V.

KING ARTHUR.

THE missionary Augustine, who went from Rome to Britain to convert the Saxons to Christianity, landed in Kent in the year 596. From that visit of his, with forty companions, the present organization of the English church is derived.

But there were Christians in Britain before Augustine. Christianity had been introduced there in the Roman Army, and so long as the Roman posts were maintained there, there were Christian churches. The native Britons had embraced some form of Christianity. The Saxons, who began to invade them as soon as the Roman garrisons were withdrawn, had no Christian faith or institutions. It is of the conversion of these Saxon intruders that we speak, when we say that Augustine and his companions converted England to Christianity.

For more than a hundred years before Augustine
came, there had been a series of incursions by
the Saxons, and of battles between them and the
Britons whom they found there.   The Romans,
with their garrisons, had kept the peace.   But,
nearly two centuries before Augustine's time, the
Romans had been so hard pressed by the warlike
tribes who invaded them, that they had been
obliged to withdraw their garrisons.   In those two
centuries the British tribes began to quarrel with
each other.   Much such a result followed as would
follow in the East Indies now, if the English army
was withdrawn.   In the midst of these disturbances
among themselves, the Saxons and Angles, from
the north of Germany, found out that Britain was
a good place to live in, and began their invasions.
They were the neighbors of the Lombards or Long-
beards, who at about the same time marched south
into Italy, whose general was Garibald, a name
which has re-appeared in another Lombard general
of later time.

In these two centuries of civil wars, and war
against invaders with very little written history, you

KING ARTHUR'S ROUND TABLE.

may be sure, and very little civilization, there
was just the chance for the growth of legends.
"What your grandfather told," and "what your
grandmother remembered," could grow in that
soil, as mushroom spores will grow if you give
them the soil they love. So that on the very
ground where yesterday you heard no story at all,
you might to-morrow hear of Jack the Giant Killer,
of Tom Thumb, of Jack and the Bean Stalk, of
the Rye Pudding, of the four and twenty black
birds, and if you were a little older, of Lancelot, of
Gawain, of Elaine, of the Round Table and the
Hundred Knights thereof.

When, in a historical mood, you look back in the
chronicles, to see what all this started from, you
do not find great comfort. Here is the confession
of Geoffrey of Monmouth, who wrote six hundred
years after the time he says Arthur died.

"Whilst occupied on many and various studies,
I happened to light upon the history of the kings
of Britain, and wondered that in the account which
Gildas and Bede, in their elegant treatises had
given of them, I found nothing said of those kings

who lived here before the Incarnation of Christ,
nor of Arthur, and many others who succeeded
after the Incarnation ; though their actions both
deserved immortal fame, and were also celebrated
by many people in a pleasant manner and by heart,
as if they had been written. Whilst I was intent
upon these and such like thoughts, Walter, arch-
deacon of Oxford, a man of great eloquence, and
learned in foreign histories, offered me a very ancient book in the British tongue, which, in a con-
tinued regular story and elegant style, related the
actions of them all, from Brutus the first king of
the Britons, down to Cadawallader the son of Cad-
wallo. At his request therefore, though I had not
made fine language my study, by collecting expres-
sions from other authors, yet contented with my
own homely style, I undertook the translation of
that book into Latin."

You see that this excellent Geoffrey was surprised that in the two best histories of England
which he knew, the great King Arthur's name was
not so much as mentioned. This is probably due
to the fact that he belonged in romance and not

in history.   The truth is, that there were, in those
ages, many kings and many lords.   Where the
Saxons landed, and made a raid, the Britons gathered and opposed them.   But gradually the Saxons made head against them, and established their
permanent colonies, exactly as, later down, their
descendants established Massachusetts, and Prov-
idence Plantations, and Maryland and Virginia in
America.   In after years, more or less was remembered of the British chieftains, and on this more
or less, all the romance writers, when the time for
romances came, hung their stories.

The "Anglo-Saxon Chronicle," one of the old
collections of annals, supplies in simple form the
most important facts for the years in which Arthur
lived, if he lived at all.   You ought to read it, to
see what history is made from.

Anno. 508.   This year Cerdic and Cynric slew a British
king, whose name was Natan-leod, and five thousand men
with him.   After that the country was named Natan-lea, as
far as Cerdicsford [Charford].

A. 509.   This year St. Benedict, the abbot, father of all
monks, went to heaven.

A. 510–513.

A. 514. This year the West Saxons came to Britain with three ships, at the place which is called Cerdic's-ore, and Stuf and Whitgar fought against the Britons and put them to flight.

A. 515–518.

A. 519. This year Cerdic and Cynric obtained the kingdom of the West Saxons; and the same year they fought against the Britons where it is now named Cerdicsford. And from that time the royal offspring of the West Saxon reigned.

A. 520–526.

A. 527. This year Cerdic and Cynric fought against the Britons at the place which is called Cerdic's-lea.

A. 528–529.

A. 530. This year Cerdic and Cynric conquered the island of Wight, and slew many men at Whit-garas-byig. [Carisbrooke, in Wight.]

531–533.

A. 534. This year Cerdic, the first king of the West Saxons, died, and Cynric his son succeeded to the kingdom, and reigned from that time twenty-six years; and they gave the whole island of Wight to their two nephews Stuf and Whitgar.

535–537.

A. 538. This year, fourteen days before the Kalends of

March, the sun was eclipsed from early morning till nine in the forenoon.

A. 539.

A. 540. This year the sun was eclipsed on the twelfth before the Kalends of July, and the stars showed themselves full-nigh half an hour after nine in the forenoon.

Now, remember that, according to Geoffrey of Monmouth, Arthur died in 542. Observe that in the Anglo-Saxon Chronicle there is not one word about him in thirty-four years before that time. Then you will understand that he could not have been the single king of all England which the romances describe.

Dr. Lingard says of him : "We know neither the period when he lived nor the district over which he reigned. He is said to have fought and to have gained twelve battles. In most of these, from the names of the places, he seems to have been opposed to the Angles in Lincolnshire, from the last, at Mt. Badon, to the Saxons under Cerdic or Cynric. This, whether it was fought under Arthur or not, was a splendid and useful victory, which for forty years checked the advance of the strangers. Per-

haps when the reader has been told that Arthur
was a British chieftain, that he fought many battles,
that he was murdered by his nephew, and was
buried in Glastonbury, where his remains were discovered in the reign of Henry the Second, he will
have learned all that can be ascertained at the present day, respecting that celebrated warrior."

It is a good deal as you might read a good history of the United States for the first half of this
century, and possibly not find the name of Tecumseh; or as you might read one of the last half
of the century which should not mention Sitting
Bull. But if, a hundred years hence, you went
among a spirited tribe of Indians, who had advanced a century toward civilization, you might
find enthusiastic accounts of Sitting Bull and of
Tecumseh preserved in ballads and stories. And
these accounts, very likely, would surpass anything
which was true in the real lives of those chiefs.

I may say, in passing, that both Tecumseh and
Sitting Bull were men quite as accomplished as
the real King Arthur was. As for weapons and
arts, they were quite in advance of him.

THE SWORD EXCALIBAR.

What King Arthur means, then, to you and me, is this. He is the Hero of Chivalry, as Chivalry conceived of a Hero, when Chivalry was at its best. Sidney Lanier's edition of Sir Thomas Malory's History of King Arthur and his Knights of the Round Table is a book all boys will like to read, and it will be an excellent introduction to the Romances of Chivalry. If you ask my advice, you will read that first. Then you can read the Welsh traditions of King Arthur which this same Sidney Lanier edited, under the title of the Boy's Mabinogion. Here is a good piece from Sir Thomas Malory:

"Now assay," said Sir Ector to Sir Kay. And anon he pulled at the sword with all his might but it would not be. "Now shall we assay?" said Sir Ector to Arthur.

"I will well," said Arthur, and pulled it out easily. And therewithal Sir Ector kneeled down to the earth, and Sir Kay.

"Alas," said Arthur, "mine own dear father and brother, why kneel ye to me?"

"Nay, nay, my lord Arthur, it is not so: I was never your father nor of your blood, but I wote [*know*] well ye are of an higher blood than I weened [*thought*] ye were." And then

Sir Ector told him all. Then Arthur made a great moan when he understood that Sir Ector was not his father.

"Sir," said Ector unto Arthur, "will ye be my good and gracious lord when ye are king?"

"Else were I to blame," said Arthur, "for ye are the man in the world that I am most beholding [*obliged*] to, and my good lady and mother your wife, that as well as her own hath fostered and kept me. And if ever it be God's will that I be king, as ye say, ye shall desire of me what I may do, and I shall not fail you."

"Sir," said Sir Ector, "I will ask no more of you but that you will make my son, your fostered brother, Sir Kay, seneschal of all your lands."

"That shall be done, sir," said Arthur, "and more by the faith of my body; and never man shall have that office but he while that he and I live."

Both Lord Tennyson and Mr. Bulwer in our time have felt that in this legend of Arthur was the best subject for a great English poem. Lord Lytton said once, that he had more hope of being remembered in another century, because he had written King Arthur, than for any fame which any of his novels would have then. But you will find it hard to buy a copy to-day, and there are good public libraries which do not contain "Bulwer's

King Arthur." I am afraid that in truth Bulwer had "to pump." That is a phrase Mr. Emerson once used to me when he was speaking of another poet. The story is difficult to follow, it is long-winded, it is not founded on the real legends.

Still there are noble passages in it. Here is Arthur's prayer when Merlin has revealed to him that

> to the Saxon's sway
> Thy kingdom and thy crown shall pass away.

Arthur cries

> O thou, the Almighty lord of earth and heaven
>   Without whose will not e'en a sparrow falls,
> If to my sight the fearful truth were given,
>   If thy dread hand hath graven on these walls
>   The Assyrian's doom, and to the strangers' sway
>   My kingdom and my crown shall pass away,
>
> Grant this — a freeman's, if a monarch's prayer ! —
>   LIFE, while my life one man from chains can save ;
> While earth one refuge, or the cave one lair,
>   Yields to the closing struggle of the brave ! —
>   Mine the last desperate but avenging hand,
>   If reft the sceptre, not resigned the brand !

But, as every boy knows, who will read these lines, the tenderness, the vigor, the simplicity and the truth of Lord Tennyson's Idyls have made men and women forget all the other poetry about King Arthur. The Idyls have been published at various times, and are not published in the chronological order of their own story. But in the later editions you will find in what order the author means that they shall be read.

"It is all good," — as —— said of ——, — no matter for that story now. It will do another time. We will take almost at haphazard the true account of Arthur's origin.

> To whom the novice garrulously again :
> "Yea, one, a bard ; of whom my father said,
> Full many a noble war-song had he sung,
> Ev'n in the presence of an enemy's fleet,
> Between the steep cliff and the coming wave ;
> And many a mystic lay of life and death
> Had chanted on the smoky mountain-tops,
> When round him bent the spirits of the hills
> With all their dewy hair blown back like flame :
> So said my father — and that night the bard
> Sang Arthur's glorious wars, and sang the King

As well nigh more than man, and railed at those
Who called him the false son of Gorlois :
For there was no man knew from whence he came ;
But after tempest, when the long wave broke
All down the thundering shores of Bude and Bos,
There came a day as still as heaven, and then
They found a naked child upon the sands
Of dark Dundagil by the Cornish sea :
And that was Arthur ; and they foster'd him
Till he by miracle was approven king :
And that his grave should be a mystery
From all men, like his birth : and could he find
A woman in her womanhood as great
As he was in his manhood, then, he sang,
The twain together well might change the world."

4204

VI.

RICHARD THE LION HEARTED.

I SUPPOSE that the romances about King Arthur were first written after knight-errantry had died out. I think people remembered the theory of Chivalry in that form — and that the detail of it, as it appeared in fact — was rather blurred by time.

But now that we come, in our list of heroes, to Richard the Lion Hearted, we come into the domain of real history. I think we may say that this was at the very prime of the time of tournaments and all the rest of those brilliant shows which make the ages of real chivalry so interesting. I think that the reason that boys of our time and country are so much interested in Richard is that he is so well described in *Ivanhoe* and in the *Talisman*. Then we are all interested in the Crusades. I think we all feel that the crusade of Richard ought to have succeeded, and would have succeeded, had it been led by one man, and not by a mass-meeting or caucus — which is to say, not led at all.

For my own part, I should like to say that I do not myself think that the time for Crusades is over. Mr. Gladstone is said to have said once, that he would like to see the Sultan sent beyond the Bosphorus, "bag and baggage." The solution of the Oriental question, which thus disposes of the Turkish government, is called familiarly the "bag and baggage" policy. I think that if I had the management of affairs for a few months, I would take the Sultan and settle him in a nice valley of Asia Minor with five hundred sheep, and a brand-new shepherd's crook. I would tell him that he was in a better condition than his ancestors were, and that he might now look out for himself. I would give similar crooks to the principal officers of his court, and let each of them have one hundred sheep, and a smaller valley. Then I would provide a decent government for Constantinople and the Ottoman Empire.

In the Crusade of the year 1190 and 1191, Rich-

ard and the Western princes had in mind a policy
not unlike this. Under the inspiration of Peter the
Hermit, the first Crusade had driven the Turkish
hordes out from Jerusalem, in the year 1099. I
was always much obliged to them for selecting a
date which is so easy to remember. These vagabonds
had only been there thirty-four years. They were
genuine savages, as ignorant of the Koran as they
were of the Bible. They had no more rights there
than a gang of Apache Indians would have in
Washington to-day, if in the reign of Frank Pierce
they had found their way into Washington and had
ruled in riot there ever since. Before their time,
for four hundred years, the country had been under
Mussulman sway, but it was the sway of Arabians,
or Egyptians, who had about as much civilization
as anybody in their times. These vagabond Turks
had none ; nor have their successors had more than
a varnish of any up to this hour.

The first Crusaders drove them out of Jerusalem,
"bag and baggage," as Mr. Gladstone says. They
established in their place Godfrey of Boulogne, as
king of Jerusalem, and there he and his successors

reigned for nearly a hundred years. A queer time they had of it, and a hard one. For if there was anything which they did not understand, it was dealing with such people as they had to do with there.

At the end of nearly a hundred years, there was a very accomplished Mussulman prince named Saladin, who had succeeded in possessing himself of Egypt. He is the Saladin whom you read of in *The Talisman*. He made it his business to sweep out the Crusaders "bag and baggage" in his turn. And in a terrible battle which he fought on the fourth of July, 1187, he destroyed the army of the king of Jerusalem, and took him prisoner. He killed the bishop who bore the Holy Cross or what they thought so. And many of the Christian soldiers thought that this terrible defeat was due to the treachery of that same Grand Master of the Templars, of whom you read in *Ivanhoe*.

This critical battle of Tiberias, which established for seven hundred years Moslem power in the holy land, ended in a conflict on that level plain, in the Mount of the Beatitudes — where the Saviour is supposed to have pronounced the blessing on the Peacemakers. Strange to say it is the crater of an extinct volcano.

The stragglers from the Christian kingdom of Jerusalem came back to Europe. To redeem the city again, the third Crusade was set on foot with the support, more or less cordial, of all the great Western princes. In this Crusade our King Richard was the first king to engage publicly.

Here is the account of his departure, given by Richard of Devizes:

The time of commencing his journey pressed hard upon King Richard, as he, who had been first of all the princes on this side the Alps in taking up the cross, was unwilling to be last in setting out. A king worthy of the name of king, who, in the first year of his reign, left the kingdom of England for Christ, scarcely otherwise than if he had departed never to return. So great was the devotion of the man, so hastily, so quickly, and so speedily did he run, yea fly, to avenge the wrongs of Christ.

He went through France to Marseilles and sailed from that port towards Syria. The French king took his army by land, because he was apt to be sea-

sick. Although Richard started from England as
early as the twelfth of December, 1189, he did not
arrive at Palestine until the day before Whit-Sunday,
1191, having been more than a year on the way.
This long delay was really due to the customs of
chivalry. [For the king could not resist the temptation of taking a personal part in every encounter
which turned up; and indeed, through the whole expedition, he bore himself more as a knight-errant
seeking for glory, than as the far-seeing leader of a
great movement. Thus he stopped on the way to settle a claim he had on the king of Sicily for the dowry
of Richard's sister. Among other things, he found
time to be married with great pomp to Berengaria,
Princess of Navarre, one of the few ladies who accompanied the expedition. I think the marriage
had been agreed upon before they started. He had a
little war with some banditti, whom the chroniclers
call Griffones, in Sicily, and seems to have beaten
them thoroughly. He took possession of the island
of Cyprus, after some hard fighting. Under his
successor in the rule of England, Mr. Benjamin
D'Israeli, Cyprus has fallen under English rule

again. Even after he had left Cyprus he fell in
with a large Saracen ship, and instead of keeping
on toward Palestine he boldly attacked her.

Though our galleymen rowed repeatedly round the ship, to
scrutinize the vessel, they could find no point of attack; it
appeared so solid and so compact, and of such strong materi-
als, and it was defended by a guard of warriors who kept
throwing darts at them. Our men, therefore, relished not
the darts, nor the great height of the ship, for it was enough
to strive against a foe on equal ground, whereas a dart thrown
from above always tells upon those below, since its iron
point falls downward.

Hence their ardor relaxed, but the spirit of the king in-
creased, and he exclaimed aloud, " Will you allow the ship
to get away untouched and uninjured? Shame upon you!
are you grown cowards from sloth, after so many triumphs?
The whole world knows you are engaged in the service of
the Cross, and you will have to undergo the severest punishment, if you permit an enemy to escape while he lives, and is
thrown in your way."

Our men, therefore, making a virtue of necessity, plunged
eagerly into the water under the ship's side, and bound the
rudder with ropes to turn and retard its progress, and some,
taking hold of the cables, leapt on board the ship. The
Turks receiving them manfully, cut them to pieces as they

came on board, and lopping off the head of this one, and the hands of that, and the arms of another, cast their bodies into the sea. * * *

But they, after a mighty struggle, drove the Turks back as far as the prow of the ship, while from the interior others rushed upon our men in a body, preparing to die bravely or repel the foe. They were the choice youth of the Turks, fitted for war, and suitably armed. The battle lasted a long time, and many fell on both sides; but at last, the Turks, pressing boldly on our men, drove them back, though they resisted with all their might, and forced them from the ship. * * * *

The king seeing the dangers his men were in, and that, while the ship was uninjured, it would not be easy to take the Turks with the arms and provisions therein, commanded that each of the galleys should attack the ship with its spur — *i. e.* the iron beak. Then the galleys, drawing back, were borne by rapid strokes of the oar against the ship's sides, to pierce them — and thus the vessel was instantly broken, and becoming pervious to the waves, began to sink. When the Turks saw it, they leaped into the sea to die, and our men killed some of them and drowned the rest. The king kept thirty-five alive, namely the admiral and men who were skilled in making machines. But the rest perished, the arms were abandoned and the serpents sunk and scattered about by the waves of the sea. If that ship had arrived safely at the harbor of Acre, the Christians would never have taken the city. But by the care of God, it was converted into the destruction of the infidel, and the aid of the Christians, who hoped in him, by means of King Richard, who by his help, prospered in war.

To give poor Richard his due, he had terrible malarial attacks all through this expedition. The King of France was as unfortunate, and finally succumbed to them. Richard scarcely landed at Acre, where the Crusaders were besieging the Saracens, before he fell sick. This is the period which readers of *The Talisman* will remember. The besieging army was itself closely watched and almost besieged by Saladin, on the hills behind the town. The princes who had arrived before Richard, were very indignant at his long delay on the route, and certainly they had some reason. But, when he and his men were landed, the attack on the city took more life. Though sick himself, he joined in it, while he directed it. Special feats of his are recorded by the chroniclers. At last, "on the Friday after the translation of St. Benedict," the Turks gave hostages for the delivery of the

Holy Cross, and of their captives, and marched
out of the city. The King of France and the King
of England entered it, "and divided everything
equally between them."

After such a success, Saladin may well have considered his cause well nigh lost ; and after he lost
the battle of Jaffa, he might, even with honor, have
given it up. But the weakness of the whole Crusade was in the division of its chiefs. The King
of France was dissatisfied and went home, leaving,
however, ten thousand men to fight in Palestine.

The battle of Jaffa, so called, is a better illus-
tration than you are apt to find in history of the
hard hand-to-hand fighting. It is described, even
to tediousness in the romances, but not very frequent in real warfare. Here is a specimen of
Vinsauf's bloody narrative :

The commander of the Turks was an admiral, by name
Tekedmus, a kinsman of the sultan. He was a most cruel
persecutor, and a persevering enemy of the Christians. He
had under his command seven hundred chosen Turks of
great valor, of the household troops of Saladin, each of
whose companies bore a yellow banner with pennons of a

different color. These men, coming at full charge, attacked
our men who were turning off from them towards the stand-
ard, cutting at them, and piercing them severely, so that
even the firmness of our chiefs wavered under the weight of
the pressure. Yet our men remained immovable, compelled
to repel force by force, and the conflict grew thicker, the
blows were redoubled, and the battle raged fiercer than before. The one side labored to crush, and the other to repel.
Both exerted their strength, and although our men were by
far the fewest in numbers, they made havoc of great multitudes of the enemy. In truth the Turks were furious in
the assault and greatly distressed our men, whose blood poured
forth in a stream beneath their blows. On perceiving them
to reel and give way, William de Barris, a renowned knight,
breaking through the ranks, charged the Turks with his men,
and such was the vigor of the onset that some fell by the
edge of the sword, and others only saved themselves by rapid
flight. The King mounted on a bay Cyprian steed, which
had not its match, bounded forward in the direction of the
mountains, and scattered those he met on all sides : for the
enemy fled from his sword and gave way, while helmets tot-
tered beneath it, and sparks flew forth from its strokes.

And so on, and so on, for page after page. Any
one but Richard would have had his fill of fighting
in these fifteen months. He defeated Saladin in

battle again and again. But he did not capture
Jerusalem. Fever after fever prostrated his strength
and at last he consented to a truce. Saladin insisted on the destruction of the fortifications of
Ascalon. But he gave to the pilgrims free access
to Jerusalem. This was, in fact, all that they asked
before the Crusades began.

Poor Richard, you know, was taken prisoner on
his way home, and his ransom was a heavy one.
Nor did things fare well with him in England.
Fighting to the last, he was killed in his forty-sec-
ond year.

For many and many a year the Christian powers,
who represent the States which united in the Crusades, have had the beggar Sultan in their keeping.
He is the "sick man," whom they condescend to
keep alive. He is the nominal lord of Jerusalem
now. But he could not hold it an hour, if England
and Germany and France and Austria and Russia
did not prefer that he should.

Possibly his star may pale some day. At the
end of some Egyptian war, some Garnet Wolseley

will be bidden to march two days inland from Joppa and take possession of Jerusalem. What Richard and Philip and Henry and the rest fought for, for years, would be done, then, in forty-eight hours, by three or four English regiments. In some such way it may be that some of our young readers will see

THE LAST CRUSADE.

VII.

BAYARD.

THE Chevalier Bayard — without fear and without reproach — is on our list of heroes.

His life was worth writing and has been well written. He is most happy in the description which always accompanies his name, which I have translated. Many a person knows him as the *Chevalier sans peur et sans reproche* — who does not know where he lived, where he fought, or to what century he belonged.

He was the son of a loyal soldier who had lost his arm in battle. His education was conducted at Grenoble, under the eyes of his uncle, the bishop of that place — the brother of Bayard's mother. How many boys who read this would be well pleased were their education as simple? " It was completed," says his biographer, " when he was twelve years old, for he had then learned to read and to sign his name, and this was learning enough for a gentleman of those days." I am sorry to add that some of them, whose writing I have seen, signed their names very badly.

When he was only thirteen, he was presented to Charles, Duke of Savoy — the ancestor of the present King of Italy. The king was pleased with the boy, and made him one of his pages. He was in company with the duke at the city of Lyons once when they met the King of France, Charles the Eighth. The king liked him also, and asked the duke to give him to him, somewhat as you must ask for a fine dog or a parrot. The Duke of Savoy did so, and thus the young fellow entered into the service of one of the first princes of his time. That is, he was at the court of Charles, while his daily employments were those of a page of the Count of Ligny — Louis of Luxembourg who was a favorite of the king.

When he was only sixteen years old a Lyonese gentleman gave a great tournament in honor of the king. The page, Bayard, was determined to

be there, but he had no horse, no arms, and no
money to buy them. A friend of his, named
Bellabre, advised him to go to his uncle — and I
am not sure but that here is the origin of that
slang phrase in which a person in need, who bor-
rows money, is said "to go to his uncle." The
uncle was goodnatured, and sent the two young
friends to his own "furnisher," with a note that
he should do for them whatever they asked. The
boys did not spare. They spent four hundred
crowns each, which was thought an enormous sum.
But the uncle was reconciled, when it proved that
the money was well spent. For the Sire de Vau-
drey himself, who had arranged the tournament,
was overcome by the unknown young adventurer,
and then when, according to the custom, with his
visor lifted at last, Bayard passed before the ladies
who looked on, they were all surprised to see
that such great success had been won by Piquet.
"Piquet" was the nickname the king had given
him, as if one should call him "Spur." The king
was the only person the young fellows had entrusted with their secret. He had not had a mo-

ment's fear for his favorite "Piquet." He said,
"God grant to you what I see beginning; you shall
be Prud-homme," by which he meant, "you shall
be recognized as a leader of men," a prophecy
which was fulfilled.

The times were the times for personal daring:
Gunpowder had not wholly put plate armor and
the customs of chivalry out of the way, but the end
of them had all but come.

I am not sure but Dumas took the idea of his
Three Musketeers from the inseparable alliance
between Bayard, his friend Bellabre, and the captain of their company, whose name was Louis d'Ars.
In 1493, they all crossed the Alps together with
King Charles, who had undertaken the conquest
of Naples. Bayard was twenty years old; and
thus began the career of fighting, which he followed
till he died at the age of forty-eight, with only very
short interruptions of the days of peace. Like
other soldiers, of that country and that time, he
had various fortunes. But in all adventure he
showed the unflinching courage which has given
him his fame; and the stories told of him are ex-

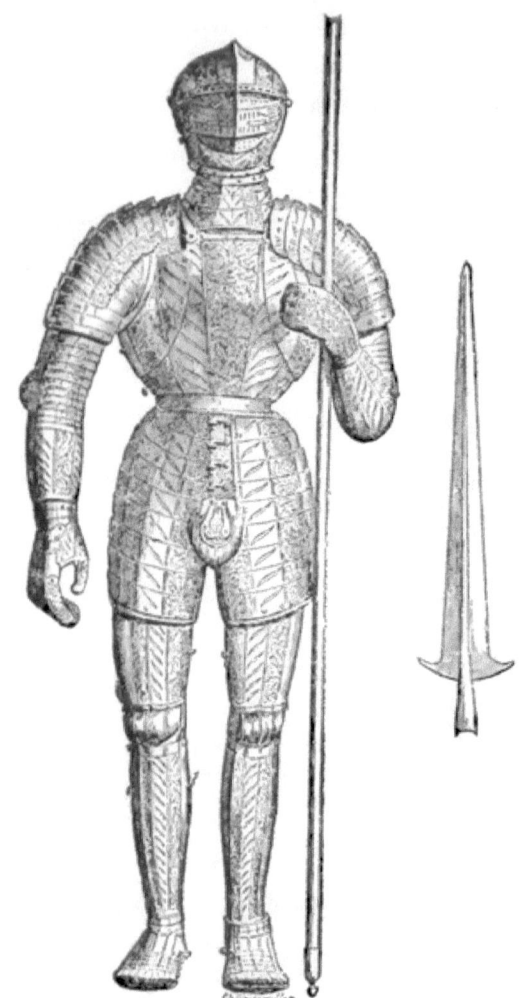

BAYARD'S ARMOR.

actly like those told in the romances of Arthur
and of Amadis.

While the French were masters of most of
Southern Italy, Bayard was made Governor of the
city of Minervino. He was always in the saddle,
as if seeking for adventure, and one day captured
a convoy of the Spanish enemy, and secured fifteen
thousand ducats. A Gascon officer claimed half
the prize, as having assisted in the capture; but
the court which heard the case refused to ac-
knowledge the claim. The man grumbled about
this, and said if he had had the money it would
have enabled him to lead an honorable life for the
rest of his days. "Is that all you need for valour
and honour?" said Bayard, and exhibited the
tempting ducats. "They are nice lozenges to
work such a cure, are they not? I see you want
to eat them, and you shall." So he gave the dis-
contented officer half the money and distributed
the rest among the soldiers.

But the end of the French occupation of Southern
Italy had come. The invasion which had begun
as a gay promenade, ended after many years of

success in a painful and laborious retreat. In this Bayard was the soul of the army.

It was at the battle of Garigliano that he repeated the achievement of Horatius. He and a gentleman named Basco, were riding a little separated from the army. Suddenly they saw a body of Spaniards who were approaching the bridge over the Garigliano, which they meant to hold against the French army. Basco rushed to warn the French. Bayard remained and held the bridge alone. The four first knights who met him "bit the dust." The Spanish leader rushed forward, sword in hand, and fell dead. "Like a tiger set free, Bayard held the bridge against them all, so that his enemies thought that here was some devil, whom they could not believe to be a man." He held it till the French arrived in force enough to drive the Spaniards back, and thus saved the army. For this gallant deed he was permitted to add the figure of a porcupine to his armorial bearings with the motto, *Vires agminis unus habet.* "Alone he has the power of a host." The Pope Julius, after this, offered to make him his general-in-chief.

THE YOUNG BAYARD ON HORSEBACK.

"I shall never have but two masters," said Bayard, "on earth the king of France, and my God in Heaven." And he returned with the army into France.

In 1510 Bayard was sent by the King of France to assist the Duke of Ferrara, some of whose dominions were claimed by the pope. The duke confided to him a plan for poisoning the pope, but Bayard was enraged, and told him he would himself inform the pope, if he did not renounce so base a scheme. In the siege of Brescia he was wounded: and after that city fell, he was carried on a litter to a house where a lady had been deserted by her husband, and was left alone with her two daughters. Bayard placed two soldiers at the door with orders to protect the house from all molestation, and gave to each of the men five hundred crowns, as his recompense for losing a share in the plunder of the city. When he was partly healed and was about to leave, the lady whom he had so served, fell on her knees before him and begged him to accept a present in token of her gratitude. Bayard smiled and asked how much the casket held which she pressed upon him. The poor woman, abashed, said, "Two thousand five hundred golden ducats, sir, but if this be not a large enough present, we will try to make it more." "No, madame," said the knight, "I do not wish any money. You have rendered me service far beyond what I could render you. I ask for your friendship and I hope you will accept mine in return." She was surprised by his courtesy, threw herself at his feet again, and said she would not rise until he accepted her present. "If you wish I will do so," said Bayard, "but am I not to have the pleasure of bidding your daughters farewell?" When the girls came, he thanked them for their care of him, and said, "I would gladly give you some token of it. But soldiers have not often jewels to give away. Your mother has made me a present of twenty-five hundred ducats. I beg each of you to accept one thousand for a dowry, and I hope you will be my almoner in dividing the rest among the convents which have been pillaged."

Gaston de Foix is said to have lost his life at the battle of Ravenna, by rejecting Bayard's advice. In 1513, when Henry the Eighth of England routed

the French in the battle of Therouenne, which took
the name of the "Battle of the Spurs" from their
rapid flight, Bayard was taken prisoner. He was
covering the retreat, at a bridge with a few companions, and when he had secured this object, he
told his friends that they must surrender. For himself, finding an English officer lying under a tree, a
little way from the battle, he spurred up to him,
pointed his sword, and said " Surrender, Sir Knight,
or you die." The officer surrendered. But Bayard
then said, " I am Captain Bayard, and I now surrender to you. Here is my sword." When a few
days after, there was talk of ransom, Bayard claimed
that the English officer owed him a ransom first.
The question was referred to the Emperor and to
Henry, who were glad to meet a soldier so distinguished as Bayard, and they recognized Bayard's
claim, and decided that the two ransoms should
offset each other.

Francis the First soon after became King of
France; he made Bayard lieutenant-general of
Dauphiny. Francis made another effort to re-con-
quer Northern Italy, and Bayard accompanied him

in the campaign. The battle of Marignan tested
the young king and his companions in arms. When
it was happily ended, King Francis asked Bayard
to confer on him the honor of knighthood, a pro-
cedure, not without precedent, but quite reversing
the ordinary custom. Bayard at first refused.

" Sir," he said, " he who has been crowned and anointed with
the oil sent from Heaven and is king of a realm, so noble,
the first son of the church, is already a knight above all
other knights." The King replied, " Bayard, be quick."
Then Bayard took his sword and replied, " Sir, it would
avail as much as if it were Roland or Oliver, Godfrey or his
brother Baudoin. Certes, you are the first king, whom
knight ever knighted — God grant you may never take flight
in war." Then looking playfully upon his sword, he said,
" Thou art right happy to have given the order of chivalry to-
day to so noble and powerful a king. Certes, my good sword, I
will keep thee as a relic, guarded above all others, and I will
never use thee except against Turks, Saracens or Moors."
Then he made two passes with it and put it back into the
sheath.

Bayard seems, however, in the course of every-
day affairs to have been no courtier. He served
his king in the saddle and in fight ; but other men

flattered him in court, amused him and took the honors. The historians agree that Francis lost his cause against Charles the Fifth, his great enemy, because he entrusted his armies to incompetent generals. It was thus that after remarkable successes in Italy he lost all but honor, as he said to his mother, in the fatal battle of Pavia in the year 1525.

But he had lost Bayard the year before. Had he not lost Bayard he might not have lost the day at Pavia.

In the campaigns by which Francis attempted once more to secure Lombardy for France, Bayard served his king most loyally, and, where he was, France succeeded. But the king had intrusted his affairs to his favorite Bonnivet, an incompetent soldier. Bayard and his troops were driven out of Genoa, and when Bonnivet finally had to retreat into France, Bayard had to play again the same part he played in his youth, when the King of France did the same thing, and cover the rear.

As the army wound along the *Val' d'Aosta*, the Spaniards attacked them; Bonnivet was wounded. Bayard again took command of the rear to save

the army if it could be saved. He put himself at
the head of the men at arms, and, animating them
by his presence and example, to sustain the whole
shock of the enemy's troops, he gained time for
the rest of his countrymen to make good their
retreat. But in this service he received a wound
which he immediately perceived to be mortal, and
being unable to continue any longer on horseback,
he ordered one of his attendants to place him under
a tree, with his face towards the enemy; then
fixing his eyes on the guard of his sword, which
he held up instead of a cross, he addressed his
prayers to God, and in this posture, which became
his character both as a soldier and as a Christian,
he calmly waited the approach of death. The Constable of Bourbon, who led the foremost of the
enemy's troops, found him in this situation, and expressed regret and pity at the sight.

" Pity not me," cried the high-spirited chevalier.
" I die as a man of honor ought, in the discharge of
my duty; they indeed are objects of pity who fight
against their king, their country and their oath."
He meant the Constable, who understood him.

The Marquis de Pescara, passing soon after, manifested his admiration of Bayard's virtues, as well as his sorrow for his fate, with the generosity of a gallant enemy; and finding that he could not be removed with safety from that spot, ordered a tent to be pitched there, and appointed proper persons to attend him. He died, notwithstanding their care, as his ancestors had done, on the field of battle. Pescara ordered his body to be embalmed, and sent to his relations; and such was the respect paid to military merit in that age, that the Duke of Savoy commanded it to be received with royal honors in all the cities of his dominions; in Dauphiny, Bayard's native country, the people of all ranks came out in a solemn procession to meet it.

Bayard died April 30, 1524. Francis lost Pavia and Italy in February of the next year.

And now why is it that Bayard is on our list of heroes?

Mostly, I think, because rare good fortune attached to him the title "*chevalier sans peur et sans reproche*," "the knight without reproach and without fear." Many a knight has deserved such an honor. Bayard had the honor given him in such phrase that men remembered it. Thousands of young Americans have deserved it better than he did. I do not think it is this particular man whom one chooses to honor or to love. But one does love this quality of courage, if it be not merely the courage of an unimaginative brute. Courage, if it be stainless courage, makes the true hero.

VIII.

ROBINSON CRUSOE.

IN our list of heroes, I have included one name of one person who was never born, and never died, and never lived with a real physical body in this world. But strange to say, this name is much dearer to most of the readers of this book than is any other upon our list. And the man to whom it belongs is much better known than are any of our other heroes.

And his name, it is " ROBINSON CRUSOE."

There are so many editions of the life of Robinson Crusoe now published, that the best informed authority on books would not even pretend to tell you what they all were, or how many. It is a book for which the demand is perfectly steady, and any good edition of it may be printed with almost a certainty that the stereotyped plates may be worn

out in printing copies which will be sold. It is a
book which is quoted among all English-speaking
people with the certainty that the quotation will be
understood. Thus, an allusion to the "man Friday," or to the footprint of the savage in the sand
would be made quite as surely as an allusion to
any familiar passage in history, or even in the
Bible.

Any people of our race would understand this
if they had ever read anything at all. Even in
such a short list of books as that of those which
Abraham Lincoln read when he was a boy, you
are almost sure to find Robinson Crusoe. Indeed,
its literary merit is such, quite apart from the human interest which belongs to almost every page,
that it would appear among the first books of English fiction, if not as the very first. Of all the stories
ever written originally in the English language, I
suppose that *Robinson Crusoe*, the *Pilgrim's Progress*
and *Uncle Tom's Cabin* have been the most widely
read.

Daniel De Foe, the author, says himself that the
whole story is an allegory with a religious purpose.

He says that it might disclose the religious experiences of a man known to him, and that it was written for that purpose. Indeed, he wrote and published a third part, devoted wholly to a Religious Vision of Robinson Crusoe. A curious book that is indeed. There is in it a picture of Crusoe outside the world — as if he were walking along the world's orbit and had been left by it. In the background you see the earth and the moon, and I think, the sun. But I speak from memory only. The book is rare and I have not seen it for many years.

Whatever may have been De Foe's intention, no one has, in fact, ever unravelled the allegory of the book. It is taken as a piece of the purest narrative in the English language, and so, in the main, I will speak of it here.

To tell Robinson Crusoe's life in brief, then, as I did Bayard's in the preceding chapter, he was born in the city of York, in England, September 30, 1632, of good family, he says. His father had been a German from Bremen, who had settled at the English seaport of Hull. So " poor old Robinson Crusoe " might have a place in the Walhalla.

The Walhalla is a splendid temple near Ratisbon, in which the king of Bavaria places busts or statues of the men and women of German race who have served the world. Among others are William the Third of England, and the great Katherine of Russia. Here he ought to put Robinson Kreutzander, otherwise Crusoe. For certainly he has done the world quite as good a turn as ever Katherine did.

Robinson was the third son of his father. He had a rambling turn and would be satisfied with nothing but going to sea — and in fact when he was but nineteen years old, on September 1, 1651, he ran away from home and took passage on a ship for London with a young friend who was going in his father's ship from Hull to London. There is not, in all the story of Robinson Crusoe, the slightest reference to the great English political struggles of the time. But it is worth while to notice that the first of September, 1651, was two days before the great battle of Worcester, in which Cromwell finally beat the Royalists and Charles the Second fled for his life. Robinson's first storm

was, apparently, on the day Charles was beaten.
Three days after, Robinson is shipwrecked at Yarmouth. This is while Charles is escaping from
England. The storm in which Robinson's ship
was lost appears elsewhere in real history.

The people at Yarmouth sent Robinson and the
others of the shipwrecked crew to London. Here
he began life, on a small scale, as a trader with
Guinea on the coast of Africa, and made one successful voyage there. In a second voyage he was
taken prisoner by a Moorish corsair, and had to
serve a Moorish nobleman as a slave. But he for-
tunately escaped with a black slave named Xury,
and was picked up by a vessel which carried him
to Rio Janeiro.

Here he became a Brazilian planter. He sent
back to London for such money as he had there,
which came out to him in well assorted English
goods. And here he might have lived and died,
and none of us would ever have heard of him, but
that he and his neighbors wanted more slaves than
they had. In an evil hour for Robinson Crusoe he
engaged in a voyage to the African coast that he

might obtain slaves for himself and his friends. The vessel, however, had not been long at sea when she was struck by a storm and wrecked on a small island at the mouth of the River Oronoco. Robinson was the only man who saved his life. On this island he lived for twenty-eight years.

The title page of the early editions is perfectly distinct as to the place of his residence. In twenty places in the book itself he states where he was. There is really no excuse for the common statement of half the school geographies and half the newspapers that he lived on Juan Fernandez on the other side of South America.

He had lived twenty-four or twenty-five years alone on his island, when on a visit from some savages who had come over from the mainland to celebrate a victory, he was able to rescue from them one of their prisoners, who became his companion and slave. Robinson gave to him the name of " Friday," from the day of his capture. In the third year after, they rescued some Spaniards and Friday's father, who had been brought over for a celebration like the other. The Spaniards had

been sent back to the mainland to bring some countrymen of theirs to .join the islanders, when an
English ship, which proved to be in the hands of
mutineers, anchored in the offing. Robinson and
Friday succeeded in rescuing the captain and
making the mutineers prisoners. The grateful
captain put the ship at his disposal, as well he
might. Robinson was eager to leave his domain,
and sailed with Friday, leaving his new Spanish
friend to his fate. He did this without hesitation.
But to us it seems that he ought to have waited.
He had been on his island, according to his own
statement, twenty-eight years, two months and nineteen days. This would make his departure from it
December 19, 1687. But his own figures say that
he left on the nineteenth of December, 1686, and
that he arrived in England, June 11, 1687. This
would give only twenty-seven years and the odd
months and days on the island.

He found that the various agents who had had
the charge of his property were willing to deal
honestly with him, and that he was a rich man.
His property in various forms was worth fifty thou-

sand pounds. In the inquiries regarding this property he went to Lisbon, and he returned through
France in winter, by a journey which proved most
perilous. He arrived in England again on the four-
teenth of January, 1683, having been gone from
England, this time, nine months.

He then married, and had three or four children.
He took a farm in Bedford and became a country gentleman, living a most agreeable life. But
in the midst of his happiness, his wife died, and
his home was broken up. He felt all a stranger
in the world. In the beginning of the year 1693,
he went to London, and there met his nephew,
whom he had brought up to the sea since his return. This nephew proposed to him a voyage to
his old island, in a ship of which he was master.
Crusoe struggled against the temptation. But he
saw no reason why he should not go, as indeed
there was none, if he could provide well for his
children, and, after a year's preparation — so much
time did the outfit for a voyage then require — he
sailed again from England on January 8, 1694–95.
It was on this voyage that he almost came to Bos-

ton. What a pity he did not! He had rescued
the crews of two vessels in great distress — and at
one moment it seemed as if they might have to
come for supplies to "Virginia or any part of the
coast of America." But alas for our fathers, this
did not prove necessary. On April 10, 1695, they
found his island, after a good deal of difficulty,
having touched at several places which were quite
wrong. The colonists had had a sufficiently hard
time, both in repelling invasion from savages, and
in putting under some of the mutineers. But in
the end law and order had triumphed. The Spaniards were living in Robinson's old castle, and the
English party in two other little colonies, with
quite a number of Indians who were, I am sorry to
say, used as slaves by the rest when they wanted
them. But there was one party of the savages
consisting of thirty-seven who lived by themselves,
on a neck of land in the southeast corner of the
island; "the most subjected innocent creatures
that were ever heard of." The Englishmen had
obtained wives for themselves in an excursion to
the neighboring islands.

With these people Robinson Crusoe left a tailor, a smith, and two carpenters, and a "general arti- ficer" whom he calls, the "Jack-of-all-trades, an ingenious and merry fellow." This man married at the island an English maid-servant whom they had picked up from one of the ships which they had relieved by the way. And Robinson left them there. He also left a Catholic priest whom they had taken from another ship, and this priest mar- ried all the men to their savage wives after fit ex- planations of the contract to them. After a stay of five and twenty days, Robinson left the island.

Alas! on the third day, as they approached Brazil, an enormous fleet of canoes surrounded the vessel when she was at anchor. When Friday was trying to communicate with them, they shot a cloud of arrows into the vessel and killed him. With a sad heart Robinson went on to the Bay of Todos Santos, and here met his old partner. They set up a sloop there, which he had brought, ready to frame, from England, and sent several more colo- nists to the islands with cows, horses, calves and swine. These people all arrived safely and Robinson received letters by the sloop from the island afterwards. At a later time he had letters once more when they were not faring well. And that is the very last that was ever heard of them.

As for Robinson Crusoe, he took passage for the East Indies with his nephew. He touched at the Cape, at Madagascar, in the Persian Gulf, and in the harbor of Bengal, as he calls it, he had a quarrel with the crew of his nephew's ship. His nephew left him there with all his goods, much as Sindbad was once or twice left alone in similar regions. But Robinson was not unused to such things. He sold his goods and bought diamonds, very good ones, so that he could carry all his estate with him. He remained there some time, and then with a friend taking ship, made a voyage to Sumatra and Siam which occupied eight months, and was successful.

A second successful voyage of five months took him to Borneo, and the Spice Islands. In the course of his speculations he bought, in good faith, a Dutch ship of two hundred tons, and he spent six years trading from port to port. But once when he was in this vessel, in the river of Cambodia, he found

out that he had made a very risky purchase. For
he had bought her of a pack of mutineers, and, at
the very moment when he learned this, five armed
boats were coming down the river to take him as a
pirate. He had but just time to hoist his anchor
and make sail when the five boats appeared. Robinson sank the leading boat, but picked up three of
her men, from whom he learned the detail of the
charges made against him. The ship was perfectly
well known, and it was supposed that he was the
leader of the mutineers.

Naturally enough he and his partner did not
dare to go back to Bengal with such a reputation.
They kept eastward, and coming into a creek in
Cochin-China, careened and repaired the vessel,
with no lack of adventures.

Persevering eastward he had the good fortune to
pick up a pilot who took him to a Chinese port
called Quinchang. And here he fell in with a
Japanese merchant who bought all his opium and
took the ship to Japan, and Robinson found himself left alone in China. In those days, however,
foreigners could travel in China; and he went by

land to Nankin, then to Pekin, and to the city of Naum, if any one can find that.

Then for sixteen days, he went through "No-man's-land" and on April 13, 1703, came out at the fortress of Argun, the first point which belonged to the Czar of Muscovy. Seven months of such travelling brought him to Tobolsk, then the capital of Siberia; and here he spent the whole winter. He made acquaintance with an exiled nobleman, and offered to carry him back to Europe. This gentleman declined the offer, but introduced his son to Robinson, who brought him successfully to Archangel, where they arrived July 18, 1704. And here they sailed for the Elbe, and Robinson staid four months in Hamburg selling his goods. His own share amounted to three thousand four hundred and seventy-five pounds, seventeen shillings and three pence.

Thence he crossed over land to the Hague, and by the packet to England, arrived in London, January 10, 1705. He says himself, that he had been absent from England ten years and nine months; but any one who makes the computation sees that will be bidden to march two days inland from Joppa and take possession of Jerusalem. What Richard and Philip and Henry and the rest fought for, for years, would be done, then, in forty-eight hours, by three or four English regiments. In some such way it may be that some of our young readers will see

THE LAST CRUSADE.

VII.

THE Chevalier Bayard — without fear and without reproach — is on our list of heroes.

His life was worth writing and has been well written. He is most happy in the description which always accompanies his name, which I have translated. Many a person knows him as the *Chevalier sans peur et sans reproche* — who does not know where he lived, where he fought, or to what century he belonged.

He was the son of a loyal soldier who had lost his arm in battle. His education was conducted at Grenoble, under the eyes of his uncle, the bishop of that place — the brother of Bayard's mother. How many boys who read this would be well pleased were their education as simple? "It was completed," says his biographer, "when he was

95

he had been absent eleven years, with the exception of two days. "And here," he says, "resolving to harass myself no more, I am prepared for a longer journey than all those, having lived seventy-two years, a life of infinite variety, and learned sufficiently to know the value of retirement, and the blessing of ending our days in peace."

And this is the last that is known of Robinson Crusoe, excepting that he died. That he died, is known by the testimony of one of his descendants, who lived to the age of manhood. This descendant, whose name is not known, wrote a ballad, of which the first verse is:

> When I was a lad
> I had a cause to be sad
> For my grandfather I did lose — O!
> I bet you a can
> You have heard of the man,
> For his name it was Robinson Crusoe.

Now Robinson's oldest child was born sometime in the year 1691. If this grandchild was born even as early as 1711, and were "a lad" old enough at four years of age to feel the sentiment of sadness on the death of a grandfather, Robinson Crusoe must have lived to the age of at least eighty-three. But of the last nine years of his life, written history makes no record, excepting the two letters he received from his island, in that time. The annals of those years are to be looked.for, and his epitaph sought, if anywhere, in the county of Bedfordshire.

Now it is quite sure that much of the interest with which we follow Robinson Crusoe is due to the style in which De Foe has told the story. It is, perhaps — it is probably — the best long piece of narrative English which was ever written. Franklin, who formed his style on the study of De Foe, approaches him I think, more nearly than any other writer. So far as the study of authors goes, I think that the narrative of these two men would be the best model we could give a foreigner. But it is not the style of the book which has given it its welcome in the world. It is the man, so imagined that we think him real, who tells so openly such a story of himself. He grows in years, and in character, before our eyes. He makes mistakes, he commits crimes, he sinks in vices — and he tells of

them.   He repents, he turns about, he reforms, he
gains strength from the Fountain of Strength —
and he tells us that just as simply.

It is not often that a book traces a hero from his
birth to the age of seventy.   A certain interest
attaches to all such books — even when they are
badly done, even if the hero move on, the same
unchanged china image, from babyhood to old
age.   The great merit of this book is that the
hero does change.   He profits by experience.   He
profits by advice.   He is a different man at forty
from what he was at thirty, as at thirty he differed
from what he was at twenty.   He is very human.

And he interests us because he does so much for
himself, and has not to rest on others.   He had
learned how to make baskets.   He had not learned
how to make pipkins, but he taught himself.   He
made mistakes about his corn, but things came right
in the end.   And he learned, before he was too far
gone, that the Universe was not his Universe, nor
the world his world.   He determined that the best
thing for him to do was to be a fellow-workman
together with God.

IX.

ISRAEL PUTNAM.

Y ES," said Enos Tait, "there is a boy's hero. He is not a hero like some people on your list, whom no boy ever heard of."

"And what do you know of Israel Putnam?" said his father, who was not very enthusiastic about "Old Put." To tell the whole truth, the most profound students of American History are not apt to be enthusiastic when his name is mentioned.

"First," said Enos bravely, "he left his plough in the furrow. I like him for that." In truth I have always observed that leaving the plough in the furrow is a manœuvre boys do not dislike — when a truly good man suggests or compels it.

"There is a picture of it in the Town Library," said Enos, "and the White Horse is beyond which Old Put is going to ride to Lexington."

"Then there is the wolf!" cried Ethelbert.

"Yes, there's the wolf. And there is his ride down the stone steps. I used to think the steps were in Boston, between Cornmill and Brattle street."

"Then there is ' P. S. P. M. He is hanged,' " said his mother. "I always liked that. I read that at school before I knew what P. S. or P. M. meant."

"I think myself," said Mr. Tait, melting a little before their enthusiasm, "that that is the best thing you have named. What is very funny is, that one of the histories alters it to, 'He is executed.' 'Old Put' could no more have spelled 'executed' than he could have danced the Redowa."

"Did he spell badly?" asked Charlotte.

"He spelled horribly — could not spell at all."

"I am sure I like him for that," said poor Charlotte, whose spelling is her very weakest point. I always encourage her by telling her that in the next century people will spell as they choose [inn the next senchury peple wil spel as tha chews].

"We will have him for a girls' hero, as well at a boys' hero," said Charlotte, well pleased.

After this we took down from the shelves :

Miss Larned's *History of Windham County*, Dawson's *Gleanings from the Harvest Field of American History*, Humphreys's *Life of Putnam*, Tarbox's *Life of Putnam*, Fuller's *Veil Uplifted*, W. B. O. Peabody's *Life of Putnam*, Swett's *Battle of Bunker Hill*, Lossing's article on Putnam in *Harper's Magazine*.

Out of these, among us, we collected the narratives from which Colonel Humphreys made the Life, from which the well-known anecdotes in the schoolbooks have been taken.

The truth is that Putnam was by no means a great man. If ever anybody was unfit to be a Major General, it was he. But he was a thoroughly courageous man, and he had the good luck to have his story told by Humphreys at a time when the people of this country were wild for heroes and stories of heroes. No story suffered in Humphreys's hands — as the boys and girls will guess who live near Horse Neck, and who have seen the terrible picture of Putnam's ride in Mr. Lossing's book in which he bounds on horseback down the hill there.

I, who tell you this story, have gone into the

Wolf's Den, and I needed no rope round my waist
to pull me out. But whether I should have gone in
were a wolf at the other end, I am not sure. More
than this, when the wolf was there, it was winter,
and the rocks were covered with ice, and were " ex-
ceedingly slippery." If I told the whole story as
Colonel Humphreys tells it it would take up all
this chapter. But here is the critical passage :

Cautiously proceeding onward, he came to the ascent;
which he slowly mounted on his hands and knees until he
discovered the glaring eyeballs of the wolf, who was sitting
at the extremity of the cavern. Startled at the sight of fire,
she gnashed her teeth, and gave a sullen growl. As soon as
he had made the necessary discovery, he kicked the rope as
a signal for pulling him out. The people at the mouth of
the den, who had listened with painful anxiety, hearing the
growling of the wolf, and supposing their friend to lie in the
most imminent danger, drew him forth with such celerity
that his shirt was stripped over his head and his skin
severely lacerated. After he had adjusted his clothes, and
loaded his gun with nine buck-shot, holding a torch in one
hand and the musket in the other, he descended the second
time. When he drew nearer than before, the wolf, assuming
a still more fierce and terrible appearance, howling, rolling
her eyes, snapping her teeth, and dropping her head between

her legs, was evidently in the attitude, and on the point of springing at him. At the critical instant he levelled and fired at her head. Stunned with the shock, and suffocated with the smoke, he immediately found himself drawn out of the cave. But having refreshed himself, and permitted the smoke to dissipate, he went down the third time. Once more he came within sight of the wolf, who appearing very passive, he applied the torch to her nose, and perceiving her dead, he took hold of her ears, and then kicking the rope (still tied round his legs), the people above with no small exultation dragged them both out together.

"You keep saying, 'Colonel Humphreys,' with a sort of sneer, papa," said Enos. "What is the matter with Colonel Humphreys."

His father acknowledged the impropriety of his sneering, and said he would try to laugh. Colonel Humphreys was first an aid of Putnam's, when he probably had to see to his spelling, and afterward was an aid to Washington. Humphreys had a certain literary turn, and is one of the early American authors, of the era after the Revolution. When Mr. Tait, Enos's father, spoke lightly of him, just what he meant was this: Humphreys had heard dear "Old Put" spin these yarns over and over again.

I believe that after General Putnam had had a stroke
of paralysis, and was living at home like a caged lion,
Colonel Humphreys went and visited him. Then
Doctor Albigence Waldo kindly sent him anecdotes
which "Old Put" had told him. From such mate-
rials Colonel Humphreys made up the *Life of Putnam* which he sent to the Society of Cincinnati
of Connecticut, and which is the reservoir for the
stories which have made him a boys' hero.

When this was duly explained to Mrs. Tait and
to Charlotte, they said that it was in this way they
preferred to have history written. It made it much
more entertaining.

In 1755, when he was thirty-seven years old,
Putnam took charge of a company of volunteers in
the Connecticut contingent which joined the English army against the French. It was in the campaigns which followed, that the adventures took
place in which he saved the magazine of Fort Edward, in which he and Durkee were so closely pur-
sued, and tumbled together into the same place of
refuge, and in which he found fourteen bullet-holes
through his blanket. Modern criticism has shown

that the blanket must have been folded when it was struck; but the Tait children agreed that one bullet which had force enough to cut through an old-fashioned home-spun blanket fourteen times, was an uncomfortable neighbor. Either this or another bullet had struck Putnam's canteen, so that the fugitives had not a drop of liquor.

When this was read from Colonel Humphreys's book, aunt Lois expressed her joy; but Charlotte explained that the danger to poor Putnam's person was the same, whether the canteen contained New England rum or water.

The war in Canada ended, virtually, by the fall of Quebec, and in 1761 Putnam was again at home. But he volunteered again in the Connecticut contingent which joined the English force against Havana. The arrival of the reinforcements from New England saved the English expedition, and the capture of Havana soon followed. Had it not been returned to Spain by the treaty of the next year, Cuba would probably now belong to the United States or Great Britain.

And now he returned to his farmer's life for

twelve years. He took part in the protests against
the use of stamped paper, which, in fact, kept Connecticut free even from the presence of a sheet of
it. He went once to Natchez, where land had
been granted to the survivors of the Havana expedition, and he sent some laborers and tools there.
Once and again he was in Boston, and met there
Gage, Colonel Small and other officers with whom
he had served in the French War. He also met
Lord Percy. With these gentlemen he had friendly
converse on the threatening state of affairs. Being once, in particular, asked, "whether he did not
seriously believe that a well-appointed British
army of five thousand veterans could march through
the whole continent of America?" he replied
briskly, "No doubt, if they behaved civilly, and
paid well for everything they wanted: but "— after
a moment's pause added — " if they should attempt
it in a hostile manner (though the American men
were out of the question) the women, with their
ladles and broomsticks, would knock them all on
the head before they had got half way through."

Meanwhile, at home, the militia were under regular training for service, and such men as he were of course chosen commanders. The news of Lexington found him ploughing — as the picture shows which Enos Tait had seen — and without changing his clothes he set out for Boston.

He was at once appointed a Major General by his own colony. As such he probably gave commands to the Connecticut regiments at Bunker Hill — where he was present. He was not the commander-in-chief, for the expedition was sent out by General Ward, who had a Massachusetts commission, and had directed Colonel Prescott to fortify the hill, which he did. Putnam had meanwhile distinguished himself in a skirmish, in which an English vessel was burned at Hog-Island; just beyond what is now East Boston. The news of this reached Philadelphia in time to quicken Congress in making him a Major-General on the Continental establishment. If Congress were to fight battles, it would not do to have a general from Connecticut, who owed no allegiance to a general from Massachusetts. On the very day that Putnam was trying to fortify Bunker Hill, to cover

the retreat of Prescott and his men who were on
Breed's Hill, Congress made him a Major-General
of the United States. It was in the same series of
appointments in which ·Washington was named
Commander-in-Chief.

When the English left Boston, Putnam was sent
to New York and assisted in the effort to defend
that city. Just before the fatal battle of Long
Island he was appointed to the command there.
The failure of the American troops has been
charged to his incompetency, but perhaps he had
not fair time to make proper arrangements to repel the attack. After this he held the command,
at one time of the posts above New York. It was
when he was in this command that he made the
Break-neck ride, and that he wrote the note, with
" P. S. P. M. He is hanged," which so pleased
Mrs. Tait for its brevity.

But, in December, 1779, the fine old fellow was
struck with paralysis which disabled him, and he
resigned his command in the army. From that
time till he died he lived in Pomfret telling his
old stories and fighting his old battles.

X.

GENERAL LAFAYETTE.

MR. FIELDS was fond of telling of his sur-
prise when a gentleman who had had
decent opportunities of education asked him one
day if he had known Mr. Pope, the poet, person-
ally.

Mr. Fields would have needed to be one hundred and thirty years old to have seen the great
poet — and as he was one of the youngest of men,
till the day he died, he was much amused at the
supposition.

Mr. Scroop was as much amused when Lucy
Flint asked him if he had known General Israel
Putnam. The dear old Wolf-Killer died ninety-
five years ago. But Lucy is not very strong in
her chronology. And, when the others laughed at
her — and Mr. Scroop tried to relieve her, by tell-

ing her that she had not been rude, as she feared
— he said, " To comfort you, Lucy, I will tell you
that I have seen the next hero on this list with
these eyes.

"It was LAFAYETTE," said he. "Marie Jean
Paul Roch Yves Gilbert Motier, Marquis de Lafayette. He has a long name, but in America, in
the army, he was affectionately known as the Marquis. And many a man was christened ' Marquis,'
in his honor, a hundred or more years ago."

In Feudal times, and before, a man who was appointed to guard the *Marches* or frontiers of a kingdom was called by a name which was eventually
corrupted into *Marquis* — and Lafayette inherited
this title.

"Now he was a boys' hero indeed," said Mr.
Scroop, "and a man's hero too."

"And what is the difference?" asked Will.

"To name no other," said his father, "I
think that boys would like, in general, to have
their heroes start early in life — and to shew that
affairs may pivot on people of sixteen or eighteen,
as well as on old statesmen of seventy-five."

"As they did when that dreadful child — in
that impossible Sunday-school story — 'pushed a
pound' in the fictitious launching, of a ship which
was never built," said Lucy.

"Do not be skeptical before your years, my
dear. At any rate you will be satisfied with Lafayette — who was wounded in the battle of Brandywine when he was younger than some of the
officers whom I have applauded in a school-drill
in the Boston Theatre."

Winifred pricked up her ears at this and began to listen. "And were you at the battle too?"
she said.

At this the others laughed heartily again, and
explained to her that the battle was a hundred and
eight years ago. To all which Winifred said that
she did not care — that she was sure Mr. Scroop had
said he had seen Lafayette — and she thought he
might have carried him from the field.

Mr. Scroop hastened to explain that he saw
Lafayette the day when the cornerstone of Bunker
Hill Monument was laid. "I was a little boy,"
he said, "three years and three months old. I had

had the scarlet fever, and was very weak. But
when the procession with the hero, passed, on its
way to the ceremony, it was wisely thought that I
should be pleased to see the show, and I was
carried to the window. The windows of the
Parker House, opposite the Tremont House, look
out on the same spot of the same street from the
same side to-day. But then there was neither
Parker House nor Tremont House."

"And how did he look, uncle John, was he
walking, or was he on horseback?"

"Or was he borne on the shoulders of men?"

"Woe is me!" cried uncle John, "I am a living
instance of the worthlessness of tradition. These
eyes have seen him. But I do not remember one
least hair of his head. I do not even remember
that I have remembered him. I do remember the
green feathers in the hats of a militia company
called the 'Rifle Rangers.' These pleased my
young fancy more than the hero did.

"Also I remember the badges with his picture
printed upon them. Some were pink, some were
blue, and some were white. And your aunt Mrs.

BARTHOLDI'S STATUE OF LAFAYETTE.

Rhoades has one this day to show if what I say be true.

"But these realities are all I remember."

"How was he wounded when he was a boy, uncle John?"

"He was wounded in the leg, and he wrote his young wife a very pretty letter about it."

"Why, was he married already?" cried almost all the boys and girls, in amazement. "Pray how old was he when he was married?" asked Robert, who was at that age when boys wonder how their fathers ever had courage to ask any girl to marry them.

Uncle John explained again that so far as this went, all the asking was probably done by somebody else. The young marquis, who did not remember his own father, was born on the sixth of September, 1757. He was at eleven placed in a school in Paris, and while he was there, his mother died. The death of her father made the young marquis a rich man. He was married at the age of sixteen. He was on duty with his regiment, in the city of Metz, a garrison town in the east of

France, when the Duke of Gloucester, a younger
brother of George the Third, came there on a visit.
The young Lafayette met the young prince at a
dinner party. The talk turned on the rebellion of
the American colonies of England. What Lafayette heard then started him upon his career. It
was the good fortune of the Duke of Gloucester to
set in motion the most efficient ally America had
in the Revolution. When Mr. Scroop told the
children this story he said :

"I do not at this moment remember anything
else which the Duke of Gloucester ever did for his
country."

Nor do I.

Lafayette was thoroughly good about coming to
help the rebels. He fitted out a ship at his own
cost, with such stores as he thought would be of
value, and sailed in her. His boy-letters to his
young wife on the voyage and afterwards are charming. He calls her " Mon cher cœur," which means,
I suppose, 'my sweetheart.' He sends pretty mes-
sages to his baby, Henrietta, whom he was never
to see again.

Since my last letter, I have been in the country which is the most disagreeable in the world, I mean the sea — for the sea is so sad, and I believe that the sea and I mutually sadden each other.

And again he says,

I am still on this sad plain, and that is certainly the most tedious thing which one can do. There is nothing tedious enough to compare with it. To console myself a little, I think of you and my friends. I think of the pleasure of seeing you again. How charming the moment when I shall come home. I shall come in suddenly to embrace you without being expected ; perhaps the children will be with you ? — I have arrived at last, my sweetheart, in very good health, and am now in the house of an American officer. By the greatest good fortune in the world, a French vessel is just ready to sail. Think how happy I am !

Here is his account of his wound at the battle of Brandywine. In the earlier letters he had explained to his poor little wife that a general officer was really in no sort of danger. He had now to confess that in his very first battle he was wounded. I observe that he wrote to her immediately, but they would not let him write a long letter. " I

begin by telling you that I am well, because I
must end by saying to you that we had a good battle yesterday, and that we were not the strong-
est." Is not that a pretty way to announce a defeat ?

Our Americans, after having held firmly for a long time,
ended by being routed. When I was trying to rally them,
the English gentlemen gave me, gratis, a musketshot which
has wounded my leg a little ; but this is nothing, my sweetheart. The ball has touched neither bone nor nerve, and I
am let off by being laid on my back for some time, which
makes me very cross. I hope, my sweetheart, that you will
not let this trouble you, for it is really a reason for being less
troubled since it will keep me out of action for some time,
because I mean to take very good care of myself. Be well
assured of this — my sweetheart.

Afterwards, he says :

Now you are the wife of an American general officer, so I
must teach you your lesson. People will say to you, " your
friends have been beaten ; " you will reply, " that is true, but
between two armies, equal in number, in an open country,
old soldiers always have the advantage over new ; besides
we had the pleasure of killing a great many people, many
more of the enemy than we lost ourselves." After this, they

will say, "that is very fine, but Philadelphia is captured, the capital of America and the bulwark of liberty." You will reply, "you're fools! Philadelphia is a sad place, of which the harbor had been closed already, and which the session of Congress had made famous. I don't know why; that is all there is about this famous town, which, in parenthesis, we will take back sooner or later." If after this they annoy you with questions, you will send them marching in terms which the Viscount de Noailles will teach you, for I am not going to take my time in teaching you politics.

Now is not that a pretty letter for one sweet-heart to write to another? He was twenty years old when he wrote it. He recovered from his wound, and he showed once and again, in very active campaigns, that he was a man of real military genius. But I am not going to tell you the story of his life, even briefly. To tell the truth, my wish has been to interest you all so much in his own way of telling it, that all of you who are sensible and bright shall go to the Public Library, shall take out the French book, and try how well you can puzzle out the French in which his letters are written. That is the true way to read history — to read it in the original authorities.

Lafayette flew backward and forward over the ocean whenever he could best help America. He was in the thick of the fight at Yorktown, and in that brilliant night attack on the two redoubts which decided Cornwallis's fate, Lafayette led the American column. He entered his redoubt first, and was able to offer assistance to the French column which had assailed the others.

In the French Revolution he kept a level head, to borrow a convenient expression from modern slang — an expression so convenient that it will perhaps assert for itself a permanent place in language. In all the "might-have-beens" with which people try to tell how the French Revolution could have done its work, without its horrors, they have to imagine it going forward on the lines of Lafayette's wishes. He was at times the most popular of Frenchmen — and at other times was most detested by the frantic Revolutionists. After he had done his best for France, he had to leave France, and the Austrians were stupid enough to imprison him at Olmutz. Here is a most picturesque bit of history. Napoleon released him. But he and

Napoleon never could work together. When Napoleon fell — and when the Bourbons fell in 1830, Lafayette's chances to serve France came in again — and he used them like a man.

But the government of the Restoration, the government to which we owe it that men now speak of an obstinate fool as a " Bourbon," quarrelled with him — and really, though not in form, sent him into exile. It was then, in 1824 and 1825, he came to America. The country received him with an enthusiasm worthy of itself and of France. The country did not know before how enthusiastic it could be. It was on this visit that he laid the corner-stone of the monument.

As you read history you will find that some men laugh at Lafayette. Carlyle, quoting Mirabeau, calls him " Grandison Cromwell Lafayette," which means that he was a revolutionist who made bows, and relied on etiquette. But if you will read carefully you will come out assured that he was no fool — that he was, as I have said, a man of real military genius — and, which is much better, you will believe him an upright and conscientious man.

XI.

NAPOLEON THE FIRST.

IT was with some hesitation that we placed Napoleon Bonaparte, the first emperor of that name, on our list of heroes. To tell the truth, I do not think he will be on such a list — a list of boys' heroes — in the year 1985. Now a hero who is not permanently or always a hero, is only a hero of the second class.

I think if any intelligent person had made a list of boys' heroes in the year 1760, it would certainly have included Frederic of Prussia — if the list had been made for American boys or English boys. He was a very successful soldier. He had been a very successful administrator. He had made a small kingdom into a very powerful one. Any young man who could, sought to obtain some post in his army. The young men, of whose private lives I know anything, in America at that time, eagerly studied what they could find of his writing and of Frederic's life.

But I am equally certain that he would be put on no list of boys' heroes now. Mr. Carlyle has put him on his list of heroes — by which he means persons who by their power of accomplishment, have lifted their heads above the current of their time. But Mr. Carlyle cannot make people believe that Frederic has a place in the lasting regard of men. I do not myself think that Frederic has left anything very important as his gift to the world. It has been said that his best gift to Germany was the introduction of the potato — and I think that would have come in without him.

Now I suppose that the fame of Napoleon the First is declining with every year, as that of Frederic the Great has declined. Napoleon was a very skil-ful person in this very important business of fight-ing. He could live with very little sleep. He had a very hard heart. He cared for nobody but him-self. He understood the business of war wonder-fully well. By instinct, almost, he brought to act

on one point the largest possible number of men,
and almost always crushed his enemy in doing so.
When a nation is at war these are great gifts.
And, by such means, Napoleon made himself
Emperor of France, and kept himself in that posi-
tion for eleven years.

But these are not gifts which through all ages
command the regard and admiration of men.
Other men appear who have the same gifts.   The
circumstances go by which made those gifts of
value.   Thus it would be very hard for me to persuade any boy or girl that it is important now to
any one, that Napoleon succeeded in the battle of
Borodino in the year 1812.   But, in the battle of
Borodino seventy or eighty thousand men were
killed or wounded — and no man can be justified in
compelling such loss of life but by some great exi-
gency.   If the objects of a man's life are transitory,
and the methods by which he gained them are
transitory, I think his fame will not be eternal or
the regard which men have for him.

In truth there are only three realities in life
which are eternal.   They are Faith and Hope and

Love. Napoleon had neither of these. For I do not think that the confidence he had in his own star is fairly to be called Hope.

Still we have put Napoleon the First, though rather doubtfully, upon our list of "boys' heroes," because every one likes to read about him, and, in our time, ought to read about him. In other times I think people will read about him as little as they now read about Charles the Bold. He lived in a country which is very enthusiastic about military success. He created a school of admirers who regarded military success as the greatest success of all. And a library of the Memoirs of Napoleon — or books bearing upon his history — is one of the most entertaining collection of books which you can find. There are such libraries. They number many thousands of volumes.

Napoleon Bonaparte was born on August 15, 1769. It seems to me a little curious that the celebration of the hundredth anniversary of his birth was not more distinguished by public celebration. It has been observed with interest that Arthur Wellesley, afterwards Duke of Wellington, who met Napoleon in battle at Waterloo, was born in the same year. He was three months and fifteen days older than Napoleon.

Napoleon, in early life, always spelt his name Buonaparte — with a *u* in the first syllable. He changed the spelling to Bonaparte without a *u*, all of a sudden. It is said that up to a certain day all the autographs have the letter *u*, that on that day there is one letter with it, and another without it, and that always afterwards he wrote it with *o* alone. I suppose that after he became a French ruler he did not care to use spelling which is distinctly Italian. He was born in Corsica, which was ceded to the crown of France in June, 1768. He was therefore born a subject of Louis the Sixteenth. Had he been born sixteen months before he would have been born a citizen of the Republic of Genoa, which held Corsica till its cession to France.

His father was a well-educated man, who was of the patriot party, as it was called, of Paoli, a person a good deal heard of in those days. It was afterwards Napoleon's duty when he was only a captain of artillery to serve against Paoli. When he was a little boy, only ten years old, he was sent to the military school at Brienne, and here he remained what was called a "king's pensioner" until he was in his sixteenth year. Observe that when he was a schoolboy in this school the boys heard of Lafayette's and Rochambeau's successes with French troops in America.

Here is his own account of his boyhood :

In my infancy I was extremely headstrong; nothing over-awed me, nothing disconcerted me. I was quarrelsome, mischievous; I was afraid of nobody; I beat one, I scratched another; I made myself formidable to the whole family. My brother Joseph was the one with whom I was oftenest embroiled; he was beaten, bitten, abused; I went to complain before he had time to recover from his confusion. I had need to be on the alert; our mother would have repressed my warlike humor, she would not have put up with my caprices. Her tenderness was joined with severity; she punished, rewarded, all alike; the good, the bad, nothing escaped her. My father, a man of sense, but too fond of pleasure to pay much attention to our infancy, sometimes attempted to excuse our faults. "Let them alone," she said; "it is not your business. It is I who must look after them."

Napoleon also tells this story of himself

I recollect a mischance which befel me in this way, and the punishment which was inflicted on me. We had some fig-trees in a vineyard; we used to climb them; we might meet with a fall and accidents; she forbade us to go near them without her knowledge. This prohibition gave me a good deal of uneasiness: but it had been pronounced, and I attended to it. One day, however, when I was idle, and at a loss for something to do, I took it in my head to long for some of these figs. They were ripe; no one saw me, or could know anything of the matter: I made my escape, ran to the tree, and gathered the whole. My appetite being satisfied, I was providing for the future by filling my pockets, when an unlucky vineyard-keeper came in sight. I was half-dead with fear, and remained fixed on the branch of the tree, where he had surprised me. He wished to seize and conduct me before my mother. Despair rendered me eloquent; I represented my distress, undertook to keep away from the figs in future, was prodigal of assurances, and he seemed satisfied. I congratulated myself on having come off so well, and fancied that the adventure would not transpire; but the traitor told all. The next day Signora Letitia wanted me to go and gather some figs. I had not left any, there were none to be found: the keeper came, great reproaches followed, and an exposure; the culprit had to expiate his fault.

Here is his account of his first journey from home :

> I still remember the tears she shed when I quitted Corsica. That is now forty years ago. You were not then born : I was young, and did not foresee the glory that awaited me, still less that we should find ourselves here together *; but destiny is unchangeable : one must obey one's star. Mine was to run through the extremes of life ; and I set out to fulfil the task assigned me. My father repaired to Versailles, whither he had been deputed by the Corsican *noblesse*. I accompanied him ; we passed through Tuscany — I saw Florence and the Grand Duke. We at length reached Paris — we had been recommended to the Queen. My father was well received, feasted. I entered the school at Brienne ; I was delighted. My head began to ferment ; I wanted to learn, to know, to distinguish myself — I devoured the books that came in my way. Presently there was no talk in the school except about me. I was admired by some, envied by others ; I felt conscious of my strength and enjoyed my superiority.

It was, of course, very curious in after times, to see what Napoleon's teacher thought of him. The following report was discovered, and made public :

* At St. Helena.

State of the king's scholars eligible from their age to enter into the service or to pass to the school at Paris; to wit M. de Buonaparte (Napoleon), born the 15th of August, 1769, in height 4 feet, 10 inches, 10 lines (5 feet 6 1-2 inches English) has finished his fourth season; of a good constitution, health excellent; character mild, honest, and grateful; conduct exemplary; has always distinguished himself by his application to the mathematics; understands history and geography tolerably well; is indifferently skilled in merely ornamental studies, or in Latin, in which he has only finished his fourth course; would make an excellent sailor; deserves to be passed on to the school at Paris.

His old master Leguille, professor of history at Paris, boasted, that in a list of the different scholars, he had predicted his pupil's subsequent career. In fact, to the name of Buonaparte the following note is added: "A Corsican by birth and character — he will do something great, if circumstances favor him." Monge was his instructor in geometry, who also entertained a high opinion of him.

M. Bauer, his German master, was the only one who saw nothing in him, and was surprised at being told he was undergoing his examination for the artillery.

Napoleon received his first commission in the French army when he was only sixteen years old. He was then appointed a second lieutenant of artillery. Observe that Lafayette was commissioned at the same age. Napoleon, you see, served under the Monarchy — when Louis the Sixteenth was still one of the most popular of kings. Not long after he was commissioned, he competed for a prize offered by the Academy of Lyons, and he won it. The subject was one prepared by the Abbé Raynal: "What are the principles and institutions, by application of which mankind can be raised to the highest pitch of happiness." Few men have had such a chance to try experiments in that direction as he had in his after-life.

The conflict between the King and the People was steadily approaching. It is said that he said, in the discussions among the officers of his regiment, " Were I a general officer I would have held by the king : being a subaltern I join the Patriots." All such stories, however, are to be cautiously received. It is certain that he did take the Patriot side. In 1792, when he was twenty-three, he be-

came a captain; it was in the next year that he
served in Corsica. The French were not successful there, the army was withdrawn, and his mother,
his brother and sisters crossed to Marseilles. It is
said that they were quite poor until Napoleon was
far enough advanced in his career to relieve them.

In the south of France, there had been more
than one district where the people, or their local
leaders, had not supported with enthusiasm the
violent proceedings of the Revolutionary Convention, and had looked with particular horror on the
imprisonment of the king. The seaport of Toulon,
which was a Royal arsenal, had declared for the
King and the Constitution of 1789, and had asked
the assistance of the English and Spanish Squad-
rons which were cruising on the coast. This assistance was given; and a garrison made up of Englishmen, Spaniards, Neapolitans and Sardinians
was thrown hastily into the city, which thus became
— though a French city — a hostile town in France.
The Convention had to besiege it and to take
it.

The Convention, at the outset, managed its mil-

itary affairs very badly, having the wretched custom
of sending what was called a Committee of Public
Safety to watch and overawe the General. Lord
Mulgrave, an Englishman, held command of the
motley garrison within. Things dragged along,
with little success for the French for some time,
when Napoleon Buonaparte, who was then only a
lieutenant-colonel of artillery, was appointed commander of the artillery in the siege. So soon as
he arrived, he found that things were wretchedly
mismanaged. More than once he had to differ
from the civilians who were sent down to watch
him and the siege. In a sally which the English
made against a French outwork, Napoleon received
a bayonet wound; and O'Hara, the English commander, was wounded and taken prisoner. This is
the same O'Hara who gave up his sword to Washington at Yorktown, when Lord Cornwallis was too
ill "in his tent" to make this sign of surrender.
Immediately after this success, Napoleon opened
a heavy fire on a post which the English called
Fort Mulgrave and the French Little Gibraltar.
He weakened it so that a French column was able

to take it by storm.   After this severe loss the
allied troops withdrew.

The notes which the committees of Paris found
in the office of the artillery department, respecting
Napoleon, first called their attention to his conduct
at the siege of Toulon.   They saw that, in spite of
his youth and the inferiority of his rank, as soon as
he appeared there, he was master.   This was the
natural effect of the ascendency of knowledge, ac-
tivity, and energy, over ignorance and confusion.
He was, in fact, the conqueror of Toulon, and yet
he is scarcely named in the official dispatches.

Still, after such success, it was a year or two before his military genius had any fair chance given
to it.   It was not till the famous day which Carlyle
calls the day of the "Whiff of Grape Shot," that
he established himself as one of the great Leaders
of the French people.   On that day, October 4,
1795, he was but twenty-six years old.   From that
time for twenty years he was the most important
man who was in any way connected with France
or her government.

I have only tried to give a sketch of his life

while he was a young man.   You will all see that in
those days he showed most of the characteristics
which gave him distinction afterwards.   I think he
also showed the limitations, which make it certain
that he can never be counted among the number
who are acknowledged to be the first of men.

XII.

RALPH ALLESTREE.

WHEN, in the beginning of this series, I and a loyal body of friends selected the group of heroes whose history the reader has followed, it was agreed by those high contracting parties that the twelfth hero should be invented by me.

This new hero is to combine all the excellencies of the other twelve and none of their vices. He is to be as gentlemanly as Arthur, and Richard, and Bayard, and Robinson, and Lafayette. He is to be as tender but not as unfortunate as Hector. He is to be as brave as Horatius and Alexander, and as successful as Napoleon and Hannibal were in their early days.

Beside this his life shall have good separate anecdotes like Old Put's. I wish I could add that, like Old Put, he was to have a good biographer.

It has also been agreed that he is to be a hero
of our time, so that any boy who reads, may go and
do likewise.

He is not to be brought up in riches, far less in
abject poverty; he is to be an American, and to
have his early education in that middle state of life
to which Robinson Crusoe was born, and which
Agur prayed for.   Like most young Americans he
is to " paddle his own canoe " from early years.

As for name — we doubted a good deal, seeing
we are making him up entirely.   For if we give
him a name of the people, there will be twenty
John Fishers, or George Bacons, or William Fos-
ters who will read this very biography, and will
think the story is written about them.   Why, there
are three E. E. Hales now on the catalogue of
Harvard College, a fourth keeps a shop for dogs in
Fulton street, and a fifth runs an express wagon in
New Hampshire.   Suppose we took that name for
the Hero's name, they might all think the parable
was written of them.   Still it is very hard to write
long of a man who has no name.   I know people

who begin a story by saying, "I have a friend, who made us a visit, and went to see a friend, who lives in Friend street. My friend's friend said to my friend that a friend of hers called on a friend " — and so on and so on. But this always confuses me, for I am slow of understanding. In sympathy with readers who resemble me, it has been determined that our Hero shall have a Name.

Our proposal was to select twenty-four unusual surnames from the Directory, and as many christian names from the list at the end of the dictionary, and to draw the two names by lot from these. Proceeding on this line, with some forcing, we came upon " Rufus Mulhall," for our Hero. But every one disliked this. He was then altered to Ralph Mulhall. Then it proved that Mulhall was not an old New England name, and that seemed desirable. So we changed him to Ralph Allestree, having found Allestree in Lechford.

RALPH ALLESTREE was seventeen years old when the war of the rebellion broke out. They rejected him because he was too young, when the volunteers appeared in Boston for the First Massachusetts

Regiment. Ralph's next best chance was to go on a farm in Vermont where his uncle lived and raised horses. It was here that he learned everything about a horse which is worth knowing, and became literally, as much of a "*chevalier*" as Bayard. But it was not till he was nineteen that he could persuade any surgeon to pass him. Then he succeeded in exactly what he wanted. He was sworn in as a private in the Fourth Massachusetts Cavalry, and from the beginning had the pleasure of serving under that White Knight of modern chivalry, Francis Washburn of High Bridge.

This is the story of High Bridge. When Lee was in full retreat in Virginia, hoping, if possible, to join Johnston in North Carolina, Ord was leading the pursuit of Grant's army, and in those critical hours made one of the great marches of modern history. At last he had to stop. But before daylight on April 6, 1865, he sent forward from Berksville two small regiments of infantry and his own headquarters escort of cavalry, under Colonel Washburn's command, to burn High Bridge. He afterwards sent Theodore Read, his chief-of-staff, to

command the little party. They were all within
two miles of the river when General Lee's cavalry,
in advance of his whole army, overtook them.

Read drew up his eighty horse and five hundred infantry,
rode along the front of his ranks, inspired the men with his
own valor, and began the battle with an army in his front.
Charge after charge was made by the chivalrous Washburn,
and at last not an officer of that cavalry party was left un-
wounded to lead the men; and not until then did they surrender. But the stubborn fight in his front led Lee to believe
that a heavy force had struck the head of his column.   He
ordered a halt — and this whole portion of his army began
entrenching; so that the rear-guard and wagon train were
delayed in their march, and this gave time for Sheridan to
come up with the flying column on the Deatonsville road.*

You see that that half-day in which those fine
fellows checked an army was the end of the war.
Read and Washburn, and Washburn's officers did
not die in vain. Lee's retreat was checked long
enough, and on the next day the notes passed
between Grant and Lee which resulted in the great
surrender.

* From " Badeau's Life of Grant."

The three hundred men who died at Thermopylæ scarcely stopped Xerxes' army for a day.

The men who fought at High Bridge gave peace to the country after four years of war. They were prisoners for less than forty-eight hours. They were never exchanged — for when those forty-eight hours were over the war was done.

Yes, it was hard enough for these fine fellows to join in the triumphs of victory. They were in the great " March Past," when for a day the united armies of Sherman and of Grant poured by the White House and saluted Abraham Lincoln — in token that War was over. But not a man of them could forget, all through the honors of that day, those brave friends whose death had bought that rejoicing. But, after this great day of jubilee, regiment after regiment was discharged and they could all hurry home.

HOME! It was Ralph's first day at home for two years. And it would not be quite home, until his father came too. But they now counted it only in weeks till the *Alert* should arrive — the little cruiser which he commanded.

And the *Alert* never came. I do not know, and
no man knows in what sea — deep down, above the
bottom and below the surface — what is left of the
Alert is tossing. And I do not know, and no man
knows, where are the bodies of Ralph's father, and
of the brave men whom he commanded. From
that day to this day Ralph has done to his mother
and his brothers and his sisters what his father
would have done if — if the *Alert* had come home.

It was eight months before the Navy people
gave her up. Then they sent a great letter to Mrs.
Allestree and said they had given up the *Alert*, and
another great letter came with an order for the
administrator of Captain Allestree's estate to sign
— on presentation of which his back pay and his
prize money would be paid, and his account would
be closed.

" I shall leave it to you, Ralph," said his mother.
" You have never decided wrong."

" I knew you would say so, mother. You said
so when I joined the Fourth. And surely all came
out well then. I will tell you what I will do. I
will be a mining engineer. There is this twelve

hundred dollars in the will, left for my education. Mr. Fletcher says it must go for that, anyway. I will go to Paris first, to the School of Mines. I will go to Freyburg next, if that is the right thing to do. I will make the money last three years. And when I come home, I will know enough " —

" To confound and confuse your poor old mother."

" To make my pretty little mother as proud as a peacock of her boy — and better than that " —

" To change lead into gold," said his mother.

" No ! better than that. I will do what any American hero should do — I will be leader and guide among the Founders of States."

" Dear Ralph," said his mother, as she kissed him, " you are your father over again. But he never founded so much as a bowling-alley. Ralph, let it be as you say."

So Ralph went to Paris. And afterward he went to Freyburg, which proved to be the best thing. And he made the money last more than three years. For he was not ashamed of his clothes. He did not need to smoke, he drank water and milk and tea

and coffee, and never touched liquor. If he trav-
elled, it was on foot. If he bought books, it was
in the People's editions. "I am a 'Child of the
Public,'" Ralph said almost fiercely, for though he
was never vain, he was proud as Bayard. He was
nearly four years older, when he came home in the
steerage. He bought a silk dress for his mother
with the sixty dollars he saved by buying a steerage
passage.

And if you want to know more of him, you must
go to the State of Franklin, and spend three months
at the capital when the legislature is in session.
I forget about the capital of Franklin, but I believe
its name is to be changed to Washburn. Anyway,
if you will go to the Sierra Hotel, or the Hotel
Sierra there, if you will hire a room for three months,
and sit every evening among the loafers, and drum-
mers, the other travellers, the legislators, and the
miners who are smoking there, you may hear stories
for all that time of Ralph Allestree, or the "Boss,"
as they will call him. These stories will show that
even while he was as young as Lafayette at Brandywine, or Alexander at Issus, he was as chivalrous

as Richard and as brave as Horatius. They will show that he is as kind to his inferiors as Robinson Crusoe, more spotless than Bayard, and as true a gentleman as Hector. He has been as much loved by his companions as King Arthur, and as successful as Hannibal and Napoleon. And if I only had the tact of Colonel Humphreys in picking out anecdotes, you would say that Ralph Allestree had been as fortunate in his biography as Old Put was.

If you ever write a biography, I advise you to write it as Plutarch wrote his. Plutarch was a fool, but in spite of this — nay, I have sometimes thought because of this — he wrote the most charming biographies which were ever written.

He does not trouble you with dates or precise versifications. Thus, he does not tell you that Coriolanus was born upon the third Kalend of January, but that somebody else thinks it was on the twelfth. You do not care a straw — no, nor the finest filament of a straw, which day he was born. Nor does anybody else in the wide world or the wider heaven. Instead of such rigmarole Plutarch tells you a string of entertaining stories. Some of

them when he wrote, had survived the wreck of
time for many centuries.   And, from these stories,
you know a great deal more of the man than you
would know by any certainty that he was born at
the village of Veii and not at the village of Peii, or
that he was inoculated by Doctor Fabius and not
by Doctor Labius, if indeed there had been any
doctors or any inoculation in those days.   I have
said this before, but I say it again.   We will tell
our story in Plutarch's way — for it is undoubtedly
the best way.

One day Ralph was voyaging on Lake Superior.
They were out of sight of land, for there was the
very slightest haze on the horizon.   The waves of
fresh water are different from those of salt water,
but this day there was nothing which you would
call a wave, only long swells which furrowed the
lake.   These were the leavings of a long northwest
storm.   Ralph was talking with some friends on
the upper deck when they heard an agonized
scream from a woman forward.   Some instinct told
him what was the matter.   He flung into the lake
the stool on which he was sitting, ran at full speed
to the very stern of the boat and without pausing

an instant sprang head-foremost into the white
foaming trail of the vessel. She was sailing ten
or fifteen miles an hour. That means, say twelve
hundred feet in a minute, and that means twenty
feet in a second. The second he had saved by his
presence of mind, saved the life of the little German boy who had fallen into the water. For the
boy rose, and Ralph rose not twenty feet from each
other, and Ralph saw him. The boy went down
slowly, but Ralph went after him and clutched him.
In two seconds more the child was squalling lus-
tily, but Ralph was working steadily towards the
floating stool, which was not far away. In less
than five minutes a boat from the steamer was
feeling its course back by the track of white foam,
and at the end of five minutes Ralph and the little
German and the stool were hauled in. Now all
this would have been madness had he not been
sure that the stool would float, or had he lost one
second of time. But, in fact, it was not madness.
It was prudence and heroism together. The story
of that promptness went with Ralph wherever he
went, and did something toward forming the confi-

dence with which people were apt to look at him even when he was very young.

Another of his swimming feats happened at the mines. Some "tender feet" had just come in to the settlement. Ralph met the father of the family, welcomed him cordially, and asked for his children.

"I told them they might go and bathe," said the father. "They need it enough after our long journey."

"Bathe!" cried Ralph, starting from his high desk, and rushing for a lasso which hung over the door. "Have they gone to the lake?" And when the frightened father said they had, Ralph called both his clerks and old Tristram and ran at five-forty speed over the half-mile from his office to the lakeside.

It was just as he had feared. Into the marble of the shore the water of the lake had cut in curious white clefts. They were so like the bath-tubs of giants that people called them "the Baths."

The three children had been tempted, as Ralph knew they would be, to bathe in the Baths. They could all swim ; they had taken hold of hands and then leaped in together. And so, when Ralph arrived, the three children were freezing to death in this cruel water. For the walls of the cleft were so smooth with the washing of ages that neither hands nor feet could get a hold. The water was not quite as cold as ice, but it was not much warmer.

The children were swimming still, but even now Hagar could hardly hold up little Polly.

" Never fear ! never fear !" cried Ralph, " it is all right. Keep her up just half a minute more." And he slipped the loop of the lasso round his own waist. The instant old Tristam came up, he took the other end of the rope, and Ralph went into the water. He could hold up Polly now, and in a minute more all three of the children were passed out and up to the men lying on their stomachs and reaching down from the rock above.

They fairly ran the children home. They poured brandy into the inside and rubbed them with horse-hair mittens on the outside, and they were all saved.

" I have known that place to be the most dan-

gerous hole in America, since I went into it myself," said Ralph.

One awful day in midwinter, when they had
fairly given up the office because it was so cold,
and all the clerks and other outdoor people had
gathered, with kerosene lamps, in a sort of Jury
work-room they had made in an old shaft, Tristam
came in, wild with excitement, with a letter. It
was dirty and wet, but still legible, if, by good luck,
Tristam could have read. But, by ill luck, Tristam
could not read. He had found the letter tied with
a bit of old crape round the neck of a dog who had
scratched and howled at the half-blocked door of
Tristam's shanty. Tristam had been nursing a
sprained ankle there.

"The wettest, dirtiest, meanest cub you ever did
see," said Tristam in explanation. "But she had
this rag round her neck 'n' I knew that meant sun-
thin'. 'N' I brought it down right away for some
of you 'tender feet' to read."

For, to Tristam's view, all men and women who
could remember any point east of Pike's Peak were
"tender feet."

Ralph tore open the letter.

Flynn's house is burnt and Junio's Junio is badly burnt and Flynn is ded   The children and Junio and all the wim-men is in my shanty   The snow is all over us   I shall put the dog through the roof   SALL WATKINS.

Ralph read it twice to the group.

" Flynn was drunk," said he, " and so was Junio, and so was Sall."

Meanwhile, he kicked off his slippers which he was wearing for comfort, and pulled on his boots. As he did so, he said, " Who will go with me ? " without looking from the ground.

" In course I will," said old Tristam.

" In course you will not, with that foot of yours," replied Ralph.   " I should be carrying you on my back before we had gone ten rods."

" I'll go," said Nahum Spalding, who was putting on his fur coat already, his boots were on.

Observe, that the wind was blowing smartly from the northwest, that the thermometer was twenty-six degrees below zero, that the depth of the snow varied from twenty feet in the drifts to nothing on the ridges, and that Flynn's was eleven miles away — a nest of wretched drunkards, as worthless as could be found on this round ball.

Neither of the other men said a word. But, as Ralph was fastening his snow shoes, a Canadian whom they called LeBosse, said, half ashamed, that he did go once on a tramp to help a fellow Mason, and that when he arrived, the people were all blind drunk and needed no help at all.

"Yer would go ef the woman wuz a man and could make the sign of distress," said Tristam, in a quiet rage.

And at this taunt, LeBosse girded on his snow shoes, and went too.

They carried on the sled two yards of canvas rolled on two sticks, with which to make shelter from the wind, two spades, a little jug of whiskey, and some hard bread.

No! There is not room enough here to tell of their false start, of their going up the creek four miles, and having to come down because there was no chance to cross it, till they were within a mile of their starting place, to tell how LeBosse sulked and turned back; how the others lost their way, and at nightfall had not found Flynn's.   How the wind failed, but the glass went down — or would, had there been any ; how, at sunrise — late quarter to eight — they found they were at the Devil's Gap, how Nahum began to talk wild here and was " clean gone," how Ralph packed him away — knowing he would sleep — in a cleft in the Devil's Den, and fastened him in with two big bowlders ; how then Ralph went on alone, and at three in the afternoon — twenty-nine hours after he started — hailed the party at Flynn's.

There has not been any smoke.   He was afraid they were dead.   No! Junio was dying.   Sal was asleep in a drunken sleep, and all five of the children, covered up by one bear skin, by the care of Matildy, the biggest of them, were asleep also. Sal had upset the jug of whiskey which contained every particle of stimulant in the house.   A little water leaked in from the roof.   There was not a crumb of food.

None of those children died, and Sal Watkins never touched whiskey again.   Three years after she married a very decent man named Ogiltree,

who saw her at Fitch. She told him her whole
story. And she has made him a very good wife.

Ralph had organzied his first mine on the Back
to Back system. This means that the capitalists,
who lived in Chicago and New York, had one third
of the profit, the undertakers had one third — they
were himself and a smelter named Geniose, and
another man who understood the market named
Gulliver, and the workmen had one third. All
wages were, by agreement, fixed at the lowest rates
at which men could live, and everybody looked to
the profits of the mine for his real compensation.
The thing worked so well at the Washburn, that
when they opened the Cinnabar they worked on
the same system, and they did the same at the
Jasper afterwards. Mining is like everything els
in life. It is the first step which costs. They had
pulled well through the worst first steps at the
Washburn and the Cinnabar, when the whole com-
munity at the Washburn was dismayed, first by
the suspicion and then by the certainty that some
very grand people from New York who were stay-
ing at the Sierra House, and were spying out the

works had come to buy the Boss off. They had
offered him, it was said, twenty thousand dollars
a year and a share in their mines if he would come
and take the charge of the Aladdin in Montana.
Then one of them, who was a little drunk, had let
out the fact that because twenty thousand dollars
would not do, thirty thousand dollars should. Every
word of which, so far as it said that such offers had
been made, was true. And the offers were made
by substantial people, who could and would do what
they promised.

Now this did not mean death to the Washburn
works or the Cinnabar. They were, in both cases,
well established. The hands liked the bosses and
the bosses liked the hands. The capitalists understood their part — that they were to be content
with their dividends and were not to interfere. If
Ralph left, still the mines would go on.

And Ralph was not, at that time, earning anything like the smallest amount named in this mag-
nificent offer — which his skill, courage, and execu-
tive ability had well deserved. He was not earning a quarter part of twenty thousand dollars.

But he said that he considered himself bound to loyal men who had trusted him with money, and to his loyal partners, the workmen, who had come in to a new plan proposed by him, of dividing profits. Nothing had been said in writing which should bind him to stay with them. But he believed that he understood the business better than any one else did, and that he could carry it on better. He certainly should be disappointed, and should think he was harshly treated, if all his workmen left him together and went off to the Aladdin or to Alaska. He was but one and they were seven hundred. But as things were, he was, perhaps, as necessary to the Washburn, as they were.

So he staid at the Washburn and the New York gentlemen looked further for an agent.

But that sort of loyalty, of man to man, helped the Washburn so much that it is long since that the Washburn people bought out the Aladdin and that is now run on the Back-to-Back system.

There were two or three wretched camps of Indians near Washburn, and one near Cinnabar. What the poor creatures were originally I do not know — Snakes, Crows, Black-feet, Diggers or what. They were in a fair way of all going to the happy hunting-grounds when Ralph appeared on the scene. Old Tristam and most of the people he had to do with, would have told you that a dead Indian was the only good Indian — and, so far as they had any "Lord," would have thanked the Lord, had they heard that there was small-pox in either of the camps.

Ralph never smoked a pipe of peace with these wretches. One or another of them would come into the town to sell venison, or other game, and it was certain that they got no bad whiskey there. Ralph rode out one day to see them. He produced some salve for two of their ponies which had some disorder. He persuaded two of the boys to take a letter for him across to the Yellowstone Reservation, and when they came back — it was only three or four hundred miles in all — he paid them well. Then he persuaded them and another to be his regular scouts and hunters, and pleased their fancy by a little bit of uniform and gold lace. He coaxed Tubal, one of his blacksmiths, to show

the boys how to handle tools ; first nothing but a
tinker's — so that they could mend a tin pail,
but in the end they could make a tin pail or
cut an old one to pieces and make it into mugs.
The Indian girls were never unwilling to earn
finery or frocks, by doing such work either in the
garden or in the kitchen, as they were set to. The
next step was when the real chief of the gang — for
it was not a tribe — were recognized as official
hunters, and had their strips of gold lace, and a
regular science of ammunition. Finally there was
a raising, one day, of a frame house, and a state
wedding, when the chief of the scouts married the
prettiest girl in the clan. Of all which, the secret
was, that the Red-skins were kept from whiskey,
that each man who chose had land of his own, that
they were kept in the open air, that no one learned
anything on compulsion, and that they had some
one a little in advance of them to think for them
till they could think for themselves.

You may read the written and printed history of
the Territory of FRANKLIN and of the State at
FRANKLIN into which it grew, and you shall not

once find the name of Ralph Allestree in any
political position. But if you will go to the town
of Washburn in the State of Franklin, you will find
that he served in every local office which the
records of that township name. He was ready to
take care of the Pound, he was ready to serve as
School Committee-man, he was a Trial Justice, he
was a Captain of the light infantry, he was one of
the trustees of the church, he was President of the
Lyceum. And if you asked any one to-day who
knows that region, whether Franklin is a Republican State or a Democratic State, he would say that
it sends Republican Senators and Representatives
to Congress, but that, as for its government, most
people would be very apt to vote as Ralph Allestree had advised.

For it is very certain in America as in the rest
of the world that

THE LEADERS LEAD.